T O
B E
A
W A R R I O R

by

Robert Barlow Fox

SUNSTONE
PRESS

SANTA FE

Sunstone books may be purchased for edcational, business, or sales promotional use. For information please write: Special Markets Department, Sunstone Press, P.O. Box 2321, Santa Fe, New Mexico 87504-2321.

First Edition

Printed and bound in the United States of America

10 9 8 7 6 5 4 3 2 1

Library of Congress Cataloging in Publication Data:

Fox, Robert B. (Robert Barlow), 1930-
    To be a warrior / by Robert Barlow Fox. —1st ed.
        p. cm.
    ISBN: 0-86534-253-9 (pbk.)
    1. Navajo Indians—Fiction.   I. Title.
PS 3556. 0947T6   1997
813' .54—dc20
                96-35851
                CIP

Published by   SUNSTONE PRESS
                    Post Office Box 2321
                    Santa Fe, NM 87504-2321 / USA
                    (505) 988-4418 / *orders only* (800) 243-5644
                    FAX (505) 988-1025

Dedicated to the Navajo Code Talkers of World War II

. . .

This story might represent the lives and experiences of
many of the Code Talkers—
all wrapped into the one fictional character of
Clay Walker, *Walks Two Worlds*.

SONG
TO A SMALL WARRIOR

Great Father of Spirits,
He is new to this world;
Its ways are strange to him.
He is different than the others.
But a wildness of the earth is in him.
And he knows the sand and sky.
The wind and rain are akin
To the red skin
That enfolds his spirit.
Tame him a little, Great Father,
But not too much—
For he is as the desert cactus flower
Which blossoms slowly.
His soul will also be beautiful
When it reaches full bloom.

—R. B. Fox

CONTENTS

BOOK ONE
THE OLD WAYS

ONE

The arrow flew swift and true, striking its mark. The rabbit tumbled head over heels three times, rolling to a stop like a limp bean bag. A trail of red dust arose from its death throes and then settled gently upon the lifeless, furry form.

"I got it Grandfather. I got it! Did you see me hit it with one shot while it was at full run?" the boy shouted excitedly, as he leaped from his pony and knelt beside his kill.

The old man, called White Horse, reigned in his horse beside the boy's pony. His silver hair hung free to his shoulders and blew in the breeze. It contrasted to the dark leathery skin which was wrinkled like the bark of an ancient juniper. A smile was on his lips.

"I saw you, my Son. It was an excellent shot, for your pony was at a full gallop also. But we must not be too joyful in the face of death, even the death of the smallest creature."

The old man dismounted in swift, sure movements, belying his seventy-eight years. He held himself erect.

"Let us stand in humility and sing the song of the rabbit. We must ask his permission to use him for food to nourish us and give us renewed strength. We are brothers to all living things. Remember that."

White Horse broke into a mournful chant. The notes lifted in the wind and echoed off silent spires, drifting through purple canyons and over red buttes and mesas. The boy joined in, mimicking the old man, learning the words and intonations quickly.

When they finished singing the song of the rabbit, they skinned and cleaned it in silence. Finally the boy spoke.

"Grandfather, is it wrong to kill?"

"Only in anger or vengeance or wastefulness. We must kill enemies who would harm our loved ones or steal our land. One must kill for food and for the preservation of his own life and the lives of his loved ones. But the proper songs must always be sung. Your father was Navajo as we are. Our forefathers often warred upon others. But your mother was Hopi. They have always been a peaceful people.

"Grandfather, some day I would like to be a warrior and go into battle and count coup upon the enemy."

The old one was silent a long time before replying quietly. "There are no more wars. There are no more warriors. . . Come, let us ride toward that canyon ahead; in it is a clear pond into which runs a cold steam. We will bathe, make fire and cook the rabbit that your skill has acquired for us." As they rode, he explained, "The old ways are gone. They are gone to the skies and to the far side of the sun where our ancestors dwell," he indicated with a sweep of his hand. "But there are ways you must learn and I will teach you. I will be your *hataalii*. . .

They were playing as of old and wore that clothing. The old man had promised the boy that for four days and four nights they would roam the deserts and live in the old ways.

The boy held the skinned rabbit over the fire on a stick, turning it slowly. Its juices popped and crackled. White Horse broke the rabbit in half, handing one portion to the boy. They ate in silence.

The moon came into the sky. The boy spoke. "Grandfather, tell me tales of the past. Tell me tales of the old ones, of the wars, the hunts, the adventures."

"Fetch our blankets from the horses first." The teller of tales began speaking softly, a dreamy, glazed appearance passing over his eyes like a veil. "Far back in the night of time existed Earth Mother and Sky Father," began the old one.

After listening to the old stories, the boy said, "It is a good life we have here. Is it not, Grandfather?"

"It is a good life," repeated the old one.

And they slept a peaceful sleep.

T W O

The boy blinked his eyes against the day and stretched. The old man already had a fire going and was cooking fry bread.

"You would sleep your life away, my Son?" he chided him. "Greeting the dawn is a mighty experience."

"I am sorry, Grandfather."

"Here, let us eat well and fill our bellies. We must ride again."

. . .

"This land we ride through is called by the White Man, the Four Corners, because they divide the earth into separate parts. This is the only spot in America where four of their states touch: Utah, Arizona, New Mexico and Colorado. This, our land, has been barely touched by time. The White Man measures too much by what he calls time."

Slowly and silently the old man and the boy rode through the endless desert enclosed by the sandstone and mystic monoliths of brilliant colors rising out of the sand. The old man spoke again, reverently. "We are a part of this land, my Son. Its red dust is in our skin. Here we have always herded our sheep. Here we will always build our juniper and mud hogans. Here our women will always weave the colors of the country into our rugs, and we will continue to hammer our songs and stories with skillful touch into silver and turquoise."

White Horse shouted, changing his tone. "Come, I will race you to that cathedral up ahead."

"You ride well, my Son," said the old man, still breathing heavily. "You just need to learn a few more secrets and you will beat me easily. Talk with your animal, encourage him. He will understand you. Let him set the pace. He too likes to compete."

"I thank you for the instruction, Grandfather."

They rode at a slower pace to cool down their horses. The old one's brow was furrowed in thought. There was a matter that he must discuss with the boy. This was the time, he decided. He asked quietly. "How much do you remember of your parents, my boy?"

A shadow crossed the boys face, changing his happy countenance to fear. He began to tremble. His memory recalled once again so vividly that night his mother had sent him for his father.

. . .

He entered the smoke filled, noisy saloon. There was a circle of men. He walked closer so he could see through their legs. It was his father and another man in the circle. A shiny object flashed in the other man's hand. It struck at his father once, twice, three times. His father fell forward on his face and blood began to puddle under him.

He remembered running until he could run no more. He hid in the hills until the cold night drove him back to the hogan where he huddled in a corner for many days and would not eat nor speak to anyone.

He remembered how his mother started getting sick and acting strangely. Then others started pointing and laughing at her and calling her bad names. Some nights she never came home. He found out that she was in a condition called drunk, which was caused from drinking the poisoned water called whiskey. Then she didn't come home anymore. . .

. . .

"Do you remember them?" the old man was asking again, bringing the boy back to the conscious world.

"I am sorry, my Grandfather. . . Yes, too well. The memories are painful. I push them back into the darkness of my mind."

"It is better that you bring them into the light where sunshine will chase them away. . . I had to know, my Son, because it is related to matters that we must discuss."

T H R E E

A far off whinny was answered by their own horses. "Wild horses, my Grandson," said the old one. "There they are. There!"

"I see them Grandfather. There are maybe ten or a dozen of them."

"Are you rested enough to give chase? We can always use more horses. Our strength is in the land and our horses."

"Yes, I am ready," said the boy eagerly.

"Forget the brood mares," shouted the old man. "It is the stallion we want."

By quick maneuvers and hand signals, they trapped the big black in a V-wedge formed by two huge sandstones. The old man sprang from his horse before it had stopped. The boy dismounted cautiously. The stallion was pawing the earth and tossing its head. The old man approached with the rope ready. "Be ready now to mount him, my Son." Not once did the old man take his eyes from the eyes of the stallion. He began talking and chanting in low tones to the beast. "When I signal, grab his mane and jump astride." He reached up with the rope and slipped it over the animal's neck. "Now!" he shouted.

The boy swung astride. The stallion sunfished, throwing his head sideways and up and down. The boy turned the animal's head sharply with the rope and took him in a tight circle, riding him into the deep sand so he couldn't buck. Finally, he gave the animal its head towards the open prairie.

It was half an hour before they returned to sight. The stallion was trotting. The boy sat proudly.

"It was a good ride," the old one said. "Tie him behind us. We must watch him and snub him down when he fights. Wild ones do not trail easily."

F O U R

They had ridden all night without stopping. The boy knew that they had been climbing higher, although he could see little in the dark. The air became colder.

"We have arrived," the old man announced. "This is our destination." When the horses were taken care of, he said, "Now come. Take my hand."

They walked a few paces. Suddenly the sun burst from its confines in the lower world. The boy caught his breath as daylight revealed that they were standing on the edge of the world. A river wound its way like a snake through the deep crevice of canyons. The Great God was present in the land. The old man took out a pouch of sacred cornmeal. He repeated sacred words and threw a handful into the winds of the four directions. Then he sang a song to the dawn.

The boy stood silent in wonderment. The presence of The Great Mystery was felt everywhere. The wind echoed like *chindi*, the voices of ghosts from the past.

"We are in the presence of the Grandfather of the skies," said the old man. "Here we can see the Sky Father and our Earth Mother at their best. Here we can look inside ourselves and seek the best that is within us. Do my words all fly above you?"

"Some of them enter my heart, Grandfather."

"It is good. I will now talk of our purpose for this moment. Your parents became weak and faltered on the earth trail because of a burden that was placed upon them. Their only son was chosen and dedicated to the *Dineh* for a mission with which they found it hard to agree."

The old man hesitated, reluctant to continue. "The name by which you are called everyday is Clay Walker. This is only your American name. I now tell you your sacred name chosen by *The People*. Your name is *Walks Two Worlds*."

Clay Walker, listened wide-eyed, as they squatted Navajo style, facing each other.

"Your name," continued White Horse, "explains your mission: Walks Two Worlds. You will learn to walk completely in two different worlds: the world of *The People*, the *Dineh*. And the world of the *belagaana*, the White Man."

He paused to ask, "Are you following me, my Son?"

"Yes, Grandfather. I understand."

"You are now in your training to walk as a man in the first of these worlds. I, your grandfather, am your *hataalii*. I am your teacher of the old ways of our people. "Before many seasons it will come time for you to enter the second world and to learn the ways of the White Man."

The boy's eyes showed fear.

"I sense your fears, my Son. But hear me. You wish to ask if you have any voice in this. I answer no to your questions. It has been decided by the council of elders. It is done."

White Horse rose wearily to his feet, the boy arising also. He placed his hand on Clay Walker's shoulder and spoke more softly. "It is often hard to be a brave boy. It is harder and lonelier to be a man. It is *The People's* hope, it is my hope, that you will walk as a man of honor in both worlds, taking unto yourself what is best and wisest from both of them."

F I V E

A cold drizzling rain was falling. Clay felt as gloomy as the day. The sheep were huddled together. He sat under a Joshua tree for what shelter it offered. He had begun to feel the full message of what his grandfather had told him. He did not want this change to destroy his peaceful existence. Change was frightening.

Rough talking voices came to his ears. Three figures were approaching. They walked crazily, using bad language. As they drew near, he saw that it was his friends, Charlie Jimenez and Big Boy George. They were with an older boy known as Chino. Trouble walked with Chino.

"Look what we have found," said Big Boy George. "There sits one who is now superior to us."

"Once he was even our friend. . .before he became changed," said Charlie.

Clay smelled their breath. It was whiskey, which explained the way they were behaving. "I have not changed and I am still your friend," said Clay sullenly.

"We know you are going to the white world," said Charlie. "Such things cannot be kept secret."

Chino put his foot on Clay's chest and pushed him over on his back. "Show us you are superior."

"Yes, show us that you are superior," repeated Charlie.

"Speak to us in the White Man's language," said Big Boy.

Clay rose to his feet and faced them. "I did not ask for this thing which I must do. The elders said it must be."

"But you are changed," continued Chino, not willing to drop the matter.

Chino pushed Clay hard. Big Boy moved behind Clay. He tried to watch them all as he kept turning slowly. They pushed him around like a limp kachina doll. Clay became angry and started pushing back. Without warning

Chino struck him and knocked him down.

A silence came over them. Clay slowly wiped blood from the corner of his mouth. Slowly he got to his feet. And then swiftly his fist shot out and caught Chino squarely on the nose. Blood spurted out.

"You will be sorry for that, superior one. Hold him, Charlie and Big Boy," he commanded.

Reluctantly they grabbed Clay's arms. They seemed hesitant because the rain was washing away the whiskey in their brains. Chino approached, wiping the blood from his face. "Now we shall see how superior he is," snarled Chino.

He drove his fist hard into Clay's stomach and the blow doubled him over. Charlie and Big Boy still held his arms. Chino brought his other fist crashing into Clay's face and blood ran from his cut lips. Again Chino hit him in the ribs and sharp pains racked his body. Bright orange colors flashed before his eyes.

"It is enough," said Big Boy.

Chino paid no heed and pulled back his fist. Before he could strike, Big Boy brought his fist down hard on the back of Chino's neck and he fell.

Charlie Jimenez let Clay fall limply to the ground, his face lying in the mud. He heard their voices fading into the distance. Then he just heard the rain.

.   .   .

Clay's head throbbed like many drums were beating inside his skull. The rain had stopped falling. The sun was drying the mud on his face, so he knew that he must have been lying there for some time. He managed to drag himself painfully to his feet. He started walking, stumbling toward his hogan. His grandfather saw him coming. He ran out to help him.

"What happened, my Grandson? What trouble has befallen you?" asked White Horse with concern.

"I fell down among the rocks," Clay lied.

"It looks like the rocks fought back at you," said his grandfather. "Come. We must treat your injuries."

S I X

It was difficult for Clay to adjust again to the routine of village life after the exciting days with his grandfather, White Horse. He had recovered from the beating Chino had given him. The long days of herding sheep dragged slowly by. Life had changed, in many ways. He now had his very own horse, the beautiful black stallion. "What is such a proud animal to be called?" he asked of the wind.

The wind answered him, *Wildness is his only name.*

That was it! This creature was free and couldn't be completely broken. He would call him Wild One.

Big Boy George and Charlie Jimenez rode up to him on their horses. Big Boy George said, "That is a very fine looking horse you have there."

Charlie Jimenez asked, "Can he run as well as he looks?"

"Let us race to the giant juniper out there and we shall see," said Clay.

They shouted, kicking their horses to full speed, streaming three trails of red dust behind them. Clay Walker and Wild One won easily.

All was not play and all was not work. He must learn all there was to know about *The People* before he ventured into the domain of the White Man, unless he could escape this duty.

. . .

Clay rode upon Wild One beside his grandfather once again. Beside them in the flatbed wagon rode his two uncles, Happy Jack and Sits By The Fire. They drove a team of grays. On the wagon, feet dangling over the edge, were three Navajo women. Their many colored petticoats and their purple and green velveteen blouses contrasted with the prairie.

His two uncles wore flat brimmed, high crowned stetsons perched upon their heads. Their hair, like the women's, was bobbed into chignons. They wore bright colored shirts tucked into well worn jeans. White Horse was dressed in similar fashion except he was hatless and wore his hair loose.

Around his forehead and tied in back was a red kerchief. Instead of western styled boots, he wore ankle high moccasins with silver dimes fastened up each side.

"It is a special occasion to which we now go," the old man was telling Clay. "It is a sacred ceremonial that is known as a Navajo Sing. Soon you will see other riders, other wagons, many on foot, coming from many directions to join with us. They all know it is time. We are going to Canyon de Chelly, one of the most ancient of places where dwells the spirits of many of our ancestors."

"My Grandfather, do you wish me to fetch you a blanket from the wagon?" asked the boy.

"Thank you no, my Son. The warmth of the horse is sufficient."

They rested on a rise. The old one took advantage to again instruct the boy. "In each direction the eye may look, to the North, to the South, to the East, to the West, Above and Below—these directions each is assigned a specific color. These you must memorize. You will also learn about the four worlds which are: Fire, Air, Water, Earth. Your uncles and myself will give you instruction during the nine days of ceremony which is called the *yeibichai*."

S E V E N

They arrived at Canyon de Chelly. It was a place of the Gods. His eyes were open to everything; his ears would hear every sound. He would touch and smell and experience, for his people now considered him almost a man and he was here to learn.

Sits By The Fire awakened him early to take him around the encampment and explain what was taking place. "There will be eight full days and nine nights of songs, prayers, chants and ceremonies," his uncle explained, as they walked around the area. All through the day Clay was instructed, meeting many of their people and visiting as they went.

Toward the end of the day his uncle said, "Come. We will now go to our camp and get ready for the night activities of singing and dancing. One of the popular dances you will like. It is the Squaw Dance. Perhaps you might see the maiden of your dreams," said his uncle, laughing until his fat belly bounced like curdled goat's milk.

· · ·

The fires pushed back just enough of the night to fill the air with an eager anticipation.

"It is very exciting," commented Clay, as he sat with White Horse, Happy Jack, and Sits By The Fire.

"Yes, and it will get more exciting," replied Happy Jack. "See, already come the dancers. They are known simply as the-group-that-sings-while-it-moves."

"Notice their rattles," continued Happy Jack. "They have gourd rattles, deer hoof rattles, and turtle shell rattles."

Now the maidens entered in a line, doing a sliding shuffle with their feet. As they moved by the fire where Clay was sitting, his eyes met the eyes of a beautiful maiden. He guessed she was near his own age. Their eyes met until she danced away. A feeling pounded in his chest and stomach like he had not known before.

Sits By The Fire observed him and laughed his booming laugh. "I believe my prediction was true. Clay Walker has seen the maiden of his dreams."

. . .

It was the fifth day of *yeibichai*. His uncle, Happy Jack, was instructing him. "The last days of our ceremonial will be dedicated to the construction and destruction ceremony of the sand paintings. There is a painting created for each day. The sand paintings are for the eyes of the Gods only or to be used for the healing of the sick. The paintings cannot be left to be desecrated."

. . .

It was *yei yiaash*, the final night of the ceremony. The Arrival of the Spirits. It was also known as the Mountain Chant or Mountain Top Way, the final and most important ceremonial of *yeibichai*. Clay sat upon the ground with his grandfather and his uncles in the center of *the dark circle of boughs*. These were spruce branches piled high in a large circle. Later at night they would be set afire for the *Final Dance* also known as the *Coral* or *Fire Dance* which would conclude the *yeibichai*.

"So much to see and hear. It is difficult for me to comprehend, Grandfather," said Clay. He noticed his Uncle Happy Jack stand and silently slip away while they were talking.

"Here they come now," announced Sits By The Fire. "It is the-group-that-sings-while-it-moves. White Horse and myself shall attempt to explain everything to you while it is happening."

Clay was thrilled as the *yei bet chai* dashed down the line whirling his little basket with sacred meal. He took handfuls of the sacred meal and sprinkled the dancers, who immediately faced the east after they were sprinkled.

Before Clay had fully absorbed this, the second God of rain and snow, *Yascelbai*, pranced into the center of festivities. He was an imposing masked God known as *Water Sprinkler*. "Where is my Uncle Happy Jack?" he asked.

"He will be back soon," answered White Horse.

"Observe the Water Sprinkler," said Sits By The Fire, diverting Clay's attention back to the dance. "He brings joy and mirth just like he brings rain."

Water Sprinkler was a tall God. His painted buckskin hood came to his shoulders and was trimmed by a band of evergreen at the bottom. There were two or three eagle feathers on top. Down his naked back was a beautiful *kirtle* of hand woven wool and a streamer of colored cloth. In his left hand he carried a sprig of evergreen. "The evergreen is a symbol of everlasting life," explained his uncle.

With this part of the ceremony ending, Clay arose and said, "I must find my Uncle Happy Jack. He cannot miss the *Final Fire Dance*."

Away from the fires he found himself among the dancers and performers. A short distance from him was Water Sprinkler. Clay watched as this God removed his buckskin hood to reveal underneath the face of his Uncle Happy Jack. He was stunned to discover that his uncle was the God *Yascelbai*. He turned and walked quickly back to the fires and seated himself again between White Horse and Sits By The Fire. "He is Water Sprinkler. My own Uncle Happy Jack is the God *Yascelbai*," he said.

Yes," said his grandfather. "Perhaps it is as well that you have learned this way. Sometimes Gods are as men and sometimes men are as Gods. This is the way it is."

Silently, without words or acknowledgement, Happy Jack slipped back to join them.

The circle of spruce which surrounded them was set afire for the finale to the *yeibichai*. The flames leaped high. The spectacle ended with performers doing magic tricks in the light cast by the flames.

The ceremony was completed. Early in the morning they would all depart for their hogans.

E I G H T

Clay and White Horse had spent another day riding together. They had been in the high country. Now they were riding back down into the red sandstone and rock. The sun was on its downward journey. Wild One began acting skittish as they rode through the rocks.

Then his grandfather's horse jumped sideways and reared on its hind legs, throwing the old man to the ground. His head struck a rock and his eyes rolled back into unconsciousness. His horse ran off into the desert.

It was then Clay saw the huge rattlesnake coiled among the rocks. It hissed as its rattles stood erect, beating out their deadly rhythmic warning. He dismounted as the snake continued to rattle. He picked up a rock and was about to smash it upon the snake's head when his grandfather regained consciousness.

Raising up on an elbow he shouted, "No! No, my Boy. Don't harm it. The snake is merely defending itself. We trespassed on its domain. Let it live."

Clay dropped the rock. The snake slithered off.

"You are hurt seriously, I fear, Grandfather," said Clay, kneeling down to help the old man. "There is a deep cut in your scalp. I must stop the bleeding."

He ran a short distance and stripped some leaves from a bush, then spit upon them and rolled them into a poultice as he had once seen his uncle do. He pressed this into the wound tightly until the blood began to clot. "What can we do, Grandfather? Your horse has run away and I fear you cannot be moved. I cannot leave you here alone to go for help. . ."

"If you can mount Wild One and then help me up behind you, I can hold to your waist and shall be all right, I think," said White Horse.

After much struggle they accomplished this. They rode until the sun came near the end of its sky journey. Tall shadows reached their fingers out upon the land. They entered the canyon where walls rose high on each side. Here was where the ancient cliff dwellers once lived far back in the night of time. Empty doors and windows looked down on them like sunken eyes watching.

White Horse had told him of this region: "Before now were the Spanish slavers. Before them were the Anasazi who dwelled in cliffs. Before them we know not."

He was brought back to the present by the sound of his grandfather vomiting. He felt the violent retching tremors from the old man's body, but pretended not to notice out of respect for him. Suddenly he heard a sickening thud as his Grandfather's body hit the ground. Terror filled his heart as he saw the old man lying in a heap. He jumped off Wild One's back and put his ear to the heart of White Horse and felt it still beating. A helplessness began to press down upon him.

Through the deepening shadows he saw two riders approaching. He thought, 'Even more evil comes upon me. Surely the Gods are against me this day.'

"Hello, Clay Walker and White Horse. We are your friends," came a shout. "It is Big Boy and Charlie Jimenez that come. We became worried when you did not return," said Charlie.

"What of the old one? What has befallen him?" asked Big Boy.

"A snake scared his horse and threw him. His head struck a rock."

"We shall make a travois upon which our horses can carry him. We must get him home to our medicine man," said Charlie.

N I N E

One of Clay's uncles went for the medicine man. He arrived within minutes. He had learned the secrets of healing from the fathers back into the night of time. His name was Many Feathers. He asked first about White Horse's injury and how it came about; then he began probing around the wound. A groan escaped from White Horse.

"Is it bad?" asked Clay.

"He has a broken head bone and he bleeds inside which is worse than bleeding outside," answered Many Feathers.

"Will he live?"

"Yes, I shall make him well," said the healing man with confidence. He donned feathered bonnet, ceremonial mask and robe, and picked up his gourd rattle. Next he lit an incense which soon pervaded the hogan. Finally he began chanting. This was the last that Clay remembered before falling asleep.

. . .

Clay awoke to a more delightful smell of fry bread and hot mutton broth. Sunshine blazed in from the hogan door. He looked up into the smiling face of White Horse. "Can it be that I am not dreaming and my grandfather is well so soon?"

"It is not to be explained in words. Belief is stronger than medicine. You acted well during this crisis, my Grandson. I owe my life to your courage."

"I had help, Grandfather," Clay said shyly, but proud of the tribute given him.

"You will do well in the White Man's world for you have courage," White Horse said.

Later in the day, Clay again herded the sheep. His friends, Big Boy and Charlie rode up on their ponies and dismounted. "We came to apologize for assaulting you," said Charlie.

"It is already forgotten. I can tell you, my friends, that I do not want to learn the ways of the White Man. I am happy here."

"What will you do?" asked Big Boy.

"I think that I might run away."

"Where is this *away* to which you will run?" asked Charlie.

Clay could find no answer.

T E N

Clay had been caught sneaking food to take with him. His plan to run away had failed.

"So you thought to escape what must be?" White Horse questioned him. It was the first time the boy had seen him angry. "Would you run away forever?" He did not wait for an answer. "The false thinking of a boy."

"I *am* just a boy, my Grandfather," Clay answered.

"But the shadow of manhood hangs over you. Much is expected of you."

"I do not wish to do what is expected."

"Nevertheless, you shall go. Tomorrow you will appear before our Council of Elders," said White Horse with finality.

The spokesman and head chief was nearly a man and a half lengths tall. He wore a large black stetson with the crown uncreased, which made his head appear to nearly bump the clouds. His name was Edwin Lame Dog.

The Council gathering was held in the open space in the center of the village, surrounded by many hogans. Everyone was sitting upon the ground cross-legged. Edwin Lame Dog called the meeting to order, and addressed Clay Walker, known as *Walks Two Worlds*.

"Boy, you will stand to face this Council composed of your people. It has been brought to our attention," said Edwin Lame Dog, "that you are avoiding your responsibilities, and that you are acting like a boy."

"I *am* a boy. Were not all of you boys at one time?"

"We have all been boys. But there comes a time when the boy in each of us must be left behind and the man must come forward. You were chosen from all of our young people for the task which lies ahead. You will live with a White family and will learn their manner of eating, sleeping, talking, thinking, and the use of their money. Some day, perhaps, you can be as good as their best."

The tall chief bowed his head. When he looked up he spoke louder and his voice seemed to speak for all of his people. "The White Eyes look at me with scorn. They call me Indian. And to them it means filth, misery, laziness and drunkenness. I answer their stares with silence. What can I say to them who know me not? They see my saddened, downcast eyes. How can they see the spirit of the Anasazi within me struggling to be free?"

All of the old ones were nodding agreement. "Yes, I am Indian. I am red man. I am earth and sky. I am animal and bird. I am stream and lake and mountain. I have walked the proud land."

Edwin Lame Dog now talked more calmly and addressed his remarks to Clay. "You are *Walks Two Worlds*. You will learn completely of both of these worlds. You will see our people who have gone to these cities unprepared. You will see them in the saloons drunken with whiskey. You will see them lying in the streets. You will see them begging and squandering the money they beg. You will see them in jails lying in their own filth."

The Council Chiefs all nodded. He added his final words quietly. "But you, *Walks Two Worlds*, shall be different. You shall show us all, Indian and White, what our people can do when given a chance. . . Now, my Son, do you see why this must be, why you must soon become a man?"

Clay Walker could only nod his head.

E L E V E N

Clay Walker had a difficult question to ask. He found the courage finally to ask it, as he, his grandfather and his Uncle Sits By The Fire, ate a lunch of beans and fry-bread.

"My Grandfather, what can you tell me of woman?"

"So you have discovered the female." I should not have neglected this part of your learning. You and I have both been too long isolated from female companionship. I have grown accustomed, but you have never known. But then this is something that each man must learn for himself. . .and it takes an entire lifetime. Why do you ask your question, my Son?"

"During the *yeibichai* and the dance of the maidens, one looked at me and smiled. A strange feeling came over me."

Sits By The Fire chuckled joyously, his huge stomach bouncing like a ripe melon. "You have felt the first pains of love."

Clay said, "Tell me then of love."

A gleam came into his grandfather's eyes, then a far away look.

Sits By The Fire said, "Your grandfather thinks of his mate." Then he addressed the old man. "Am I not right, White Horse?"

"Yes. You knew her well. Was she not a fine wife to me and a truly good woman?"

"She was all that one man could ask in a woman, my friend."

White Horse looked into his grandson's searching eyes. "You never knew your grandmother. She was a beautiful, loyal companion. She was taken from me by death before her time. . .I mourned her for many moons until I became near unto sickness of the mind. I now have you to be with me, my Grandson. . .Now tell me of this maiden who seems to have captured your heart. What name is she called by?"

"She is called Rose My Only Daughter, but has chosen wisely to be known as Rose Yazzie," said Clay.

Sits By The Fire laughed heartily. "You are already thinking like a White Man when you find humor in our names. Have you spoken with the Rose Yazzie?"

"We have spoken twice with our eyes."

"And have you spoken with words?"

"Yes. Once."

"And what did you say to her?"

"Hello."

"And what did she say to you?"

"Hello."

"Do you not think that is a rather limited relationship to call love?"

"I am asking about love. How will I know when love comes?" asked Clay.

"You will have a bad pain in your belly. You will not be able to eat. You will not wish to sleep. You will be like a sick sheep." Sits By The Fire laughed again.

"What your uncle is saying," interjected White Horse, "is that you will simply *know* when love comes. The love that endures through time must be tested by black clouds of adversity as well as the joy of dancing breezes in spring. You must see your mate bear the pain of childbirth. She must see you suffer fear for the safety of your family. Then you can truly say, *I love*. Perhaps the gods of love shall smile upon you, that you might get to know this Rose-My-Only-Daughter."

T W E L V E

Rose came riding up nonchalantly. She reigned up her pinto horse and dismounted. She wore a green velveteen blouse and long purple skirt. Her raven hair hung down to the middle of her back. Her eyes were dark and teasing. She smiled at Clay, a thing most maidens would not dare to do openly.

Clay was tending his family's sheep as he did on most normal days. "Why do you not tie your hair in a chignon as the other women do?" he asked.

"Because it makes one look old, and I am young. I have lived among the Americans for two Winters and they wear their hair loose." She sat beside him. She spoke again. "Our ways are good. But they are old ways, dying ways. Maybe they should be left to the past and forgotten."

"I do not like such talk."

"Your true name is *Walks Two Worlds*."

He looked surprised that she knew.

"I have heard the old ones talking. . . You shall soon go to live among the White Ones."

"I do not wish to go."

"That is a good reason to go. You have only known one way. There are many other ways."

After a time he said, "Come. Let us ride on our horses. My cousin Harry Goldtooth can watch the sheep and goats for me." He waved to Harry, sitting in the grass a distance off, indicating that he was leaving.

They rode in silence. Clay Walker did not know what to say to a girl, but he was glad that Rose was with him. He did not look at her, but made a song which he began to sing, for he had a way of putting thoughts into songs. He sneaked a glance at her when he had finished singing. She was smiling. Then he shouted, "I will race you," and they were off.

The girl was a good rider, but Wild One was faster. She reigned her horse up beside him. "That is a fine horse you have," she said after catching her breath.

They got off their horses and walked toward the shade of the cliffs. She brushed softly against him as they sat down among the red rocks. Her touch sent strange feelings through him.

"I liked your song you sang to me. You are a very different person. You are untouched. The White Man's world will ruin you."

"I do not want to go," he repeated.

"Then why will you go?"

"It has been decreed by the Council and by my elders."

"And you always do whatever you are told to do? I am sorry," she added. "I have a rebellious spirit. . . Will you and your grandfather come to eat with us this night at our hogan?"

"I will consult my grandfather. I am sure he will agree."

"Come then. If we hurry there will be just enough time for me to help prepare the meal."

FOURTEEN

Yearly, in the spring, the young men leave their hogans and go singing toward the mountains. They go in search of their true selves.

Clay was troubled as of late. He did not wish to go to the cities of the White Man and yet he felt obligated to do so. Passions welled up within him for Rose Yazzie. Conflicts tore him apart. He thought upon the proverb his grandfather had recited to him: *Who sees the Morning Star shall see more, for he shall be wise.* He knew what he must do. He must go to the mountain to meditate and to see the Morning Star.

He would stay upon the mountain three days and three nights. He would fast. He would sleep upon the ground and wear only a loin cloth.

Beginning his assent up Blue Mountain, he observed all living things with new eyes. All of the earth lived and breathed and had a pulse of its own. His mind cleansed itself of all bad thoughts. He was preparing his spirit and his body to sing the old songs and to receive wisdom.

Wild One found the path, even in the dark of night. After many hours of riding, the summit of Blue Mountain was reached. The world of night stretched out below in all directions. He dismounted and let Wild One free to graze nearby.

The moon arose from a mountain far to the east. The night world was no longer a world of vague shadows. It became a world of moving creatures and singing night birds that made only a ghostly flutter as they flew. Even the rocks seemed to be speaking and the grasses whispering. Clay became lonely for human contact. His loins ached to be with Rose.

Suddenly he was made aware of his purpose again and rebuked himself for his weakness. He was overwhelmed by weariness and his spirit was carried into the world of dreams.

On the second night, he weakened and slept again.

On the third night he stayed awake and saw the morning star as others began to fade. He felt a moment of great peace within his soul.

When Clay rode into his village he was very weary, but this time his grandfather did not scold him, nor did he ask where he had been.

White Horse asked, "What did you see?"

Clay answered, "The Morning Star."

"And what did you hear?"

"I heard the wind; the birds spoke with me; the crickets sang for me. I heard the breath of all living things.

"What did you learn?

"I learned what I am. I learned of myself."

Softly his grandfather touched his head. "It is good," was all he said.

FIFTEEN

The long days with the sheep became lonely. The skies were gray. The winds howled their songs. But there were the days when Rose Yazzie was able to sneak out to be with him. These were warm days, no matter the weather, for they would huddle together in a blanket. They would talk or sit in silence, or share some smoked meat and dried fruit. Then time would be as fleeting as a butterfly that rests on a flower, and then flickers out of sight.

Clay hadn't thought upon his future until Rose said to him, "I shall miss you when you go to the White World."

"What is this *miss* that you speak of?"

"It means that I shall be lonely without you. It means that I will wish that you were with me."

"Then I shall miss you also, Rose."

They touched hands and then lips, according to the White Man and Woman's way of showing love.

Someone was shouting at them from a distance and was running towards them.

"It is my cousin Harry Goldtooth. I wonder why he is so excited?" said Clay.

"Clay, Clay Walker," he was yelling. "Come. Come quickly. It is your grandfather. He is very ill."

"But he was well when I left him this morning."

"All that I know is he now lies ill. The medicine man is with him."

Clay was stunned. He left, running with his cousin, forgetting to even say goodbye to Rose.

· · ·

He entered the darkness of the hogan. It took several moments for his eyes to see. He heard the chanting and the gourd rattles of the medicine man and smelled the pungent odors of the herbs. White Horse lay on his back, his lips parted and his eyes staring at something no one else could see.

Clay waited impatiently for the medicine man to finish the chant, then asked, "My grandfather, what is the matter with him?"

"He is dying. No one can help him," said the medicine man.

"What do you mean, dying!" said Clay angrily.

"He wants to die."

"White Horse does not want to die," shouted Clay. "He is a happy man."

The medicine man became angry. "Are you still the boy and not the man? Do you not yet understand the old ways that your grandfather has been trying to teach you?

"Because I say that White Horse wants to die, I do not mean that he wishes to die. I mean that death is already with him. He sees the *other side*. It is his time to die. He accepts it. . . Now go to your grandfather. Listen! for he may have a last message for you."

Clay knelt beside White Horse. Here was the only parent, the only teacher he had known. And now he was near death. Clay had never considered that this was possible. His grandfather's lips were moving.

Twice the old man repeated, "I have walked the proud land. I have walked the proud land."

Then he reached out to take death's hand, and left on the journey from which he could never return.

S I X T E E N

White Horse was buried with the honor and respect due him. His body was laid to rest in the red earth he loved so well, along with a few of his earthly possessions.

As custom required, a hole was cut into the side of his hogan so that his *chindi*, spirit, might escape to travel to the other side. Clay Walker mourned his grandfather's passing long after tradition required. White Horse had been the dominant presence in his life.

But time was here in the present. The world remained. He must find purpose to his living. His purpose would be to fulfill his grandfather's wishes for him. He would leave this land to seek his destiny in the world of the White People. He would become *Walks Two Worlds*.

. . .

His Uncles, Happy Jack and Sits By The Fire would be coming for him soon. They had purchased an old pickup truck to take him to the railway station at Thompson.

Clay Walker had rolled his few belongings into a blanket and tied it with a rope. He took a last look around the hogan. It was cold and empty now, but he felt the spirit of White Horse lingering still, and wondered at the closeness of the world of the dead and the world of the living. He picked up his blanket roll and walked outside.

He breathed deeply of the brisk air. His heart felt as though it would tear itself to shreds. He knelt upon the ground, raising his hands to Sky Father and began to sing his last song before departing.

The truck was coming. It had only one headlight piercing the dark. The truck stopped beside him and he threw his blanket roll into the back where many people were sitting. He was happily surprised to see Rose Yazzie and her parents. His friends Charlie and Big Boy were there. He was honored to see Edwin Lame Dog, the chief of his people, the tall one whose head touched the clouds. Happy Jack was driving and Sits By The Fire was next to him. Clay sat in between them.

"Where did you get this truck?" asked Clay.

"We bought it from a rancher in Kayenta," said Sits By The Fire. "It had been sitting in his pasture. He said that if we could make it run we could buy it cheap. We made it run."

Happy Jack took a final turn on the dirt trail and emerged onto the highway. He pushed down on the gas pedal. "This truck goes pretty good, huh."

"Are you sure the truck will hold together at this fast speed, Uncle?" Clay asked.

"Yeah. I am pretty sure it will."

Someone in the back of the truck began pounding on the window. Sits By The Fire turned around to see what they wanted. Then he saw the red light and the police car.

"Happy Jack," said Sits By The Fire, "I believe there is a policeman who wants us to stop."

"Then I will do it."

The truck rattled to a stop. The trooper pulled up behind them and got out of his car. He walked to the pickup and leaned on the window by Happy Jack. "I have been trying to get you to stop for the last five miles. I know you couldn't hear my siren because without a muffler your truck was roaring like a locomotive. But didn't you see my red light?" asked the police officer.

"No, I didn't see it. I was looking straight ahead to drive," answered Happy Jack.

"Don't you ever look in your rear view. . . . Oh, I see you don't have a rear view mirror. Have any of you been drinking whiskey?" he asked.

"No!" answered Sits By The Fire indignantly. "We are not drinking Indians."

"I believe you, or I would have smelled it. Let me see your driver's license, Chief," he addressed Happy Jack.

"I am not the chief. He is the tall one in the back. . ."

"Okay. Okay. Let me see *your* driver's license."

"I do not know of this driver's license. This is the first time that I drive," said Happy Jack smiling.

"You're not being smart with me, smiling about all of this, are you?" asked the officer.

Sits By The Fire explained. "He is not being bad to you, officer. He always smiles like that. No matter what happens to him, he always smiles. It is just his way."

"Okay then, smiling one, what about your license plates and inspection sticker?"

"Policeman, I tell you the truth. We did not have time to do those things. We bought this truck and are in an important hurry to take my nephew to the train. He is going to live with a White family up there in Salt Lake City," said Happy Jack proudly.

"All right. I give up," said the state trooper, tearing up the ticket he was writing. "Try to drive slower will you please." He walked back to his police car, shaking his head.

S E V E N T E E N

Thompson Railway Station was like any other small railroad spur: yellow and brown ticket office and a cafeteria attached. The pickup sputtered to a stop. Someone jumped down from the back and undid the wire holding the cab door closed, and everyone got out and stretched.

"We will now eat," announced the tall chief.

They had their lunches packed in cardboard boxes, which they carried inside the cafeteria. They lined up to get soda pops from the ice machine. People gave them patronizing stares.

A train whistle sounded down the track. The chief announced, "It is time. We will go outside."

The steaming metal monster arrived.

The chief presented Clay an envelope. "It is all arranged, my Son. You will live with a Bennett family in Salt Lake City. Their name, address and telephone number are here, in case you get lost. They are to meet you at the station. These are your train tickets and some American money to get you clothing of the White Man. There are what they call depression years taking place in the land of the *balagaana*. They say this means that they do not have enough money or jobs for their people. We have always had depression in our land." They all laughed.

Lame Dog looked into Clay's eyes. "May the Gods travel with you, my Son."

Clay stepped before each of his friends. To Big Boy George and Charlie Jimenez he said, "You have admired my horse, Wild One. You are my friends and will take care of him. He is now yours."

Next he stopped before his uncles and shook their hands. Awkwardly he faced Rose's parents. Her father spoke.

"We have relented, as you can see, and have agreed that you and Rose have been good for each other. We pray that courage may travel with you to your new world."

Last, he faced Rose Yazzie. She took both of Clay's hands in hers. "You are so good. I fear for you in the White World," she said.

"I do not fear. I shall try to honor our people by doing well. I shall miss your friendship, Rose My Only Daughter," he said.

"Perhaps we shall meet again. I am returning soon to the White Man's cities to work to make money," said Rose.

"Perhaps," he replied.

Then *Walks Two Worlds* turned to enter the train, leaving behind his old world and entering a new world he knew nothing about.

BOOK TWO

Walks Two Worlds

EIGHTEEN

The iron monster growled and screeched to a stop. They were waiting for him on the platform. Father, mother, boy about his age, girl a little younger, all very white. He hurriedly looked at the slip of paper in his shirt pocket. He couldn't read much, but remembered well. The Glen Bennett family. He felt all wrong being here. They were rushing toward him.

"You must be Clay Walker," said the father thrusting forth his hand.

Clay had been instructed that this was how White Men greeted one another. He stuck out his hand limply, like he did for the grandmothers to wind their wool yarn around.

"First thing you have to learn," said Glen Bennett, "is to grasp a hand firmly. And you must look people in their eyes. Try it again." Glen Bennett squeezed Clay's hand harder until Clay began to squeeze back. "That is much better," said Bennett. "How old are you? I wasn't sure from the correspondence."

"Fourteen, maybe fifteen. Not sure."

"You don't look that old. We'll feed you plenty and put some growing on you. Meet your new family. This is my wife, my son Mark and my daughter Ruthy."

"Hi," said Mark sarcastically.

"It is such a pleasure to meet you," said Ruthy. "It will be neat to have you as a foster brother."

Clay wondered what a foster brother was. Mrs. Bennett gave him a hug.

"Come on. Let's all get in the car and take you to your new home, Clay," said Glen Bennett. "Is this all you have?" he asked, looking at the dirty blanket tied in a roll.

"Have money to buy clothes," Clay said, handing him the money in an envelope.

Mark and Ruthy were whispering to each other. He sat in the back seat between them. Out of the corner of his eye he saw Mark hold his nose with his thumb and forefinger. The car pulled into a long gravel driveway lined by Poplar trees. The house was large.

Mrs. Bennett announced, "Clay can have the bathroom first and take a nice hot bath while I fix us a special dinner. Mark will show you your very own room, Clay, and then to your bath."

Mark led Clay down the hall, opened the door and mimicked his mother. "Your very own room, Clay." Then another two doors down. "This is the bathroom, so you may now take a nice hot bath before Mother calls us for dinner."

Clay stood bewildered, not moving.

"That is the bathtub," said Mark, pointing. "Haven't you ever used one before?"

"No. Have not seen one of those," said Clay.

"This tap is hot; this one is cold. Here are the towels to dry yourself with. There is the soap in that tray. Ever used soap?" asked Mark with a smirk.

"No. Not this kind."

"He has never even seen a bathtub," said Mark to Ruthy out in the hall.

When Clay came out of the bathroom, Mrs. Bennett called from the dining room. "Are you ready, Clay? Dinner will be served in a couple of minutes."

Clay couldn't believe his eyes: carved table, covered with a white linen cloth. Shiny dishes with painted flowers on them. Silver instruments to eat with. Rose Yazzie had been right. The *belagaana* did have all she had described.

"You can sit right here by Ruthy, Clay," said Mr. Bennett. There were a half dozen eating utensils surrounding his plate.

Ruthy saw his bewildered look. "You really only need one or two to eat with, but Mother has put out her guest dinnerware especially for you. It is really ridiculous to have so many. Watch me and you will catch on."

"Tomorrow is Saturday," said Mrs. Bennett. "I will take you shopping for some clothing, Clay. What kind of trousers do you like?"

"What is trousers?"

"You know, pants, jeans."

"I heard about levi. My uncles have some."

"Levis it will be. And maybe some sport shirts."

Mrs. Bennett wore a gold necklace with a beautiful red stone pendant that caught Clay's eye. He looked at it several times.

"Do you like this necklace, Clay?" she asked when she saw it had caught his fancy. "It belonged to my grandmother."

"Yes. I like. We have silver and turquoise."

"Yes, I noticed your beautiful ring."

"My grandfather, he made it," said Clay. Then he concentrated on his food.

When dinner was over and Mrs. Bennett suggested that he get a good nights rest, and escorted him to his room. It had a too-soft bed and a dresser with a mirror. He had seen his image reflected in water but never a mirror. It was like seeing a stranger staring out at him. There was a bookcase with magazines and books, but he couldn't read much of the *belagaana* writing. There was a closet but he didn't have much to hang in it.

He could hear Mark and Ruthy whispering out in the hall. Mark said, "I don't like him. He stinks even after a bath, and he doesn't speak English very well."

Ruthy said, "Well, he isn't English. He is American Indian. I bet you can't speak his language. Besides, I think he is rather nice."

"Well I just plain don't like him and don't trust him. I heard that you just can't trust Indians," said Mark defensively.

Clay closed his ears to their talk. He lay on top of the bed without undressing. Soon he was asleep.

NINETEEN

Mrs. Bennett took him shopping as promised, and bought him more clothes than he thought he could wear in a lifetime.

Driving home she asked, "Don't you think we should get you a haircut, Dear?"

"What you mean, haircut?"

"To have a barber trim your hair shorter. You will fit in better with the other boys and girls."

"No! My people not have short hair."

So Mrs. Bennett did not mention it again.

. . .

Sunday, they all went to church. To Clay, the singing was loud and abrasive, accompanied by a loud instrument called an organ. People stared at him. He was glad to get out of the *belagaana* church.

On the way back to the Bennett house, Mrs. Bennett asked, "Has anyone seen my necklace? I wanted to wear it to church. I must have misplaced it."

"I think I might just know where it is, Mother," said Mark.

"Oh, where, Dear?"

"I saw Clay take it into his room."

Mr. Bennett turned around and gave Mark a sharp look. "That is a serious accusation, Son."

When they got home, they found the necklace in Clay's top drawer.

"Did you think you could steal this and get away with it, Clay?" asked Glen Bennett.

"Maybe Clay has an explanation," said Mrs. Bennett.

Clay looked away. "Don't know how it is here," he said.

They closed his door.

"We cannot keep him here," said Glen Bennett.

"But dear, he was just fascinated by the necklace. Can't we give him another chance?"

"No! He cannot be trusted. We would have nothing but trouble with him in our house. I will call the federal authorities first thing in the morning. It just won't work out like we had hoped."

.   .   .

A federal officer came the next day to pick Clay up.

Ruthy's eyes were red from crying. "Daddy!" she blurted out. "I can't keep quiet about this. My conscience would not let me. Mark put the necklace in Clay's room."

Mr. Bennett shot Mark a look of anger. "Is this true, Mark?"

Tears welled up in Mark's eyes attesting to his guilt.

"Mark! I can't believe that my own son would do such a low deed. Clay, I humbly apologize for my son. I am sorry we acted so hastily. . .You may still stay with us if you wish. . ." His voice trailed off weakly.

"No! Not like you peoples."

The federal officer said to Clay, "Son, you have two choices. I can return you to the reservation or take you to the Reform School in Ogden. Which will it be?"

"Can't go home. Have disgrace my people."

On the hour drive to the Reform School in the city of Ogden, Clay Walker was silent.

TWENTY

The Indian boy stared at the stranger sitting behind the huge desk. "Sit down, Son. I am Ted Jacobs," he said. "I will be assigned as your caseworker while you are with us. Any problems that arise or questions you might have—or if you just want to talk—I am here to help. What is your name, Son?"

A paralyzing fear gripped him so he stared sullenly at the floor.

"I have to know your name, Son," persisted the stranger called Jacobs.

"Quit call me son," Clay blurted out. "I not anybody son."

"Okay. Just tell me your name."

"Clay Walker my name."

"Look, Clay, I want to be your friend, so don't fight me."

Jacobs got up from behind his desk and walked into the reception room where the federal officer was processing Clay.

"Hello, my name is Jacobs," the tall man said. "I am a Social Worker here at the school."

"Tingey's the name," said the other man. "I am with the Bureau of Indian Affairs. Here are the boy's records, Mr. Jacobs. Not much to them. He was sent to live with a Bennett family in Salt Lake City. It didn't work out. I think he is taking a bum rap. He was wrongly accused, but that is not my business. He wouldn't go back to the reservation. . . Said he had disgraced his people. . . No relatives other than a couple of uncles. So here is the only place for him until he is older, I guess."

Ted Jacobs came back into his office. "Clay Walker, I won't keep you any longer for now. I'll send for Mr. Kelly and you can go with him to get some clothing and be assigned to your living quarters. There are rules and restrictions here, though you do have some freedoms. You will learn those rules in your living quarters. I will want to talk to you later."

TWENTY-ONE

Mr. Kelly was big and fat. He was supervisor of the group-living quarters where Clay was being assigned. He had a baby-face, with black animal eyes close together. A cruel mouth seemed to smile with revenge at the world. His black hair came to a point on his forehead. His shirt never quite stretched around his fat stomach.

"Come with me, Kid," he said in a high pitched voice. "I'll just poke you inside the quarters for now. I got more important things to do."

Clay's new home had a fancy sounding name: State Industrial School; but that didn't fool him. It was still Reform School, a *belagaana* jail for kids. He was assigned to Group A living quarters, which was for older boys, although he didn't qualify by age or size.

The Utah State Industrial School was located on the outskirts of the city of Ogden in the northern part of the state. It was on a spreading acreage that stretched out at the foot of the Wasatch Range of Mountains. The institution was almost self-sustaining from its fertile farm land and livestock.

Clay Walker was conscious of all the strange faces staring at him as he plunked his belongings down inside of Group A living quarters. He was greeted by chiding remarks from the hostile appearing strangers.

"Looks like a new clod straight from the sticks."

"A little one, ain't he. Wonder why they stuck him with us. He should be with the children in Group C."

"Man, he is farther out than sticks. Dig the acres of hair and them duds he's wearing."

A redheaded kid stepped forward and stood in front of him. He was tall and skinny. His pointed nose, yellowish eyes and a shock of red hair that stuck straight in the air, reminded Clay of a turkey. His face and arms were splotched with freckles.

"I am Rusty Red. I am the big cheese around here when the boss is gone," said the redheaded one.

"And who boss is?" asked Clay.

"Slopjar Kelly is boss. He is Group A supervisor. He is big and fat and meaner than a wild bull."

"Oh. I meet him."

"Hey gang, dig that lingo he speaks."

"Yeah, it's straight from a corny western movie."

Clay felt the anger rising once more, but swallowed and said nothing.

"Slopjar said we were getting a new kid and asked me to get you a bunk and locker. Bring your gear and follow me," said the redhead.

Clay picked up his belongings and felt the eyes follow him. They entered a doorway at the back of the room and went up a flight of stairs to the sleeping quarters. It was a long, narrow room, lined with double-decker bunk beds on each side. The beds were all stretched tight with a khaki colored blanket. Behind each bunk was a metal double locker. Many of the lockers were badly battered. Some of the doors wouldn't shut, but the clothing inside was hanging neatly. The floor down the center of the room was worn like a dirt path. It was old oiled wood.

"This is the sleeping area," said Rusty Red. "No one gets in here except to sleep. Got it?"

Clay acknowledged with a grunt. They walked between the rows of beds and stopped before the end bunk on the right. "This is yours, the one on the bottom. See that you keep it neat. The end locker is yours. You got ten minutes to get squared away, then be out in front for evening roll call and chow."

T W E N T Y - T W O

Outside, the boys of Group A stood at attention in two long ranks, all except Rusty Red, who because of his status, stood in front facing them. Next to him, clipboard in his hand, stood Slopjar Kelly. Clay fell in ranks at the end of the back row just as his name was being called for the second time.

"Walker. . .Walker, the Redskin," drawled Slopjar.

"I here," he shouted.

Slopjar stopped and looked up from the clipboard. "It is *Here, Sir*, Redskin. I am group supervisor and I am *Sir*. Don't you forget that for one minute."

The two ranks turned left and marched to the mess hall. It was a large room filled with tables and benches. The entire three hundred and fifty-seven boys and their group supervisors all ate at once. Each boy at some time served on kitchen duty. The food was served in large bowls. Clay hadn't seen so much food ever in *Dinetah*. There was hot, steaming baked potatoes, real butter, hard rolls, fresh milk, all he could drink, giant lima beans in thick sauce, and fresh peaches and cream for dessert. At least he would eat well here.

Clay glanced around the dining room and noticed Slopjar Kelly at the next table. It hit him suddenly how the man had acquired his nickname. Slopjar was drinking from a pitcher of milk and it trickled from the sides of his fat lips. In his right hand he gripped a tablespoon from which he shoveled beans into his mouth from a family sized bowl. The man ate like a beast.

The groups again lined up and marched back to their living quarters. Clay was issued his regulation clothing, which consisted of two pairs of dungaree trousers; two blue denim shirts; one denim jacket; work shoes known as crap kickers or clod hoppers; standard undershorts and shirts, and a half dozen pairs of wool socks.

Sleeping quarters were opened and he stowed his clothing in his locker.

The bunk above him belonged to a retarded boy with a small pointed head, frog eyes and horse teeth, who answered to the name of Bung Jackson. He was also Clay's locker partner. Bung was harmless, although built like a bear. He talked constantly and was likeable, except for being annoying at times.

"Hi, Injun Kid. Glad to know you. I'm Bung Jackson. I really shouldn't be here. I'm not too smart and I am here mostly because no one wants me. I never had no mother that I know of. My old man was ashamed of me and didn't love me because I'm so dumb, so he sent me here to the Raft."

The Raft was the name the boys gave to the State Industrial School because it was isolated from the city and because the inmates floated on it temporarily.

"Yeah, my old man always said, `Howard, you are such a stupid jerk. Why don't you get out of here. You eat too much.' That's what my old man used to say to me. Now I know I ain't too bright up here," he continued, pointing to his head. "But I don't think I'm stupid either."

"Why you here, then?" questioned Clay.

"Well. . ." stammered Bung. "There was that one bad thing. These bad girls older than me picked me up in a car. They said they were going to neck and love with me. Them was bad girls and I wasn't about to let no necking get started because I'm pretty bashful around girls. So I started to choke a couple of them until another one clouted me on the head with a tire iron. All I saw then was a lot of colored sparkle. The judge and none of them fellahs believed me. Because my old man didn't want me, they sent me here to the Raft."

The bunk next to Clay's was occupied by a deaf mute named Arthur Diller. Clay admired Arthur's muscular body as he stripped for bed. Clay had never seen such a marvelous body on one so young. Bung saw Clay looking at Arthur and tapped the deaf mute on the shoulder.

"Injun, this is Arthur Diller."

They nodded at each other.

"Old Arthur don't belong here either," Bung rattled on. "He can't hear, can't talk, but he *knows*. He reads what your lips say. Don't you Arthur?"

Arthur gave Bung a broad smile of acknowledgment.

"Like I says, old Arthur don't belong here either, but no other place would take him. They think he is dumb like me. He is just dumb because he can't talk, but he is smart in lots of things. He got kicked out of the deaf school because he kept putting his arms around the lady teachers. He used to scare them half to death. Golly sakes, he wouldn't hurt them. He just wanted to communicate a little bit with them. You wouldn't hurt anyone really, huh Arthur?"

Arthur shook his head.

"Good criminy, Little Injun, ain't no one ever been around to help him, except when I came along to be his friend. I saw you looking at how strong Arthur is. He lifts weights and builds his body every day."

Clay was rescued from Bung's chatter when an effeminate, pale boy introduced himself. "I'm Lester Privett. They call me Pimple Face because I have an acne problem. I've got the bunk next to you."

"Lights out," came a voice from the other end of the room. Everything was suddenly darkness.

Clay lay staring at the bottom of the bunk above him, thinking of all that had happened to him in such a short time after leaving his Navojoland. Tears filled his eyes. They finally came after he had controlled them for so long.

. . .

He bolted upright in his bunk. "Gawk, gawk, gawk," a strange bird sound. Goose flesh tingled the back of his neck. He spoke in a whisper. "Who there? Who it is?"

It came again from the darkness near his bed. "Gawk, gawk, gawk," followed by a flapping sound.

Clay shouted. "Turn on lights! Somebody turn on lights!"

The the room was flooded with light. Bodies rose sleepily from bunks. In the aisle squatted Arthur Diller with his arms flapping like some awkward bird trying to fly, accompanied by weird bird sounds.

"That's just Arthur, you stupid Indian. He does that every night," shouted someone.

"What's the matter, Injun, think we got ghosts and goblins in here," taunted another. "Turn off the lights. Let a guy get some sleep."

Clay crawled sheepishly back under the covers. How he hated the Raft.

T W E N T Y - T H R E E

"Rise and shine! Time to get with it."

Clay didn't know where he was at first, and then it hit him: The Raft.

Two large feet suddenly dangled before his face. Bung Jackson rumbled to the floor, full of chatter. "Hi, Little Injun. That was some joke on you last night, huh? About old Arthur crowing and flapping his wings, huh? I bet you were pretty scared. You will get used to it and sleep right on through like the rest of us.

"Old Arthur, he don't mean no harm. It is just his habit to do that. No one knows why he wants to be a bird, unless he just wants to fly away. Hurry up, Clay. We only got a few minutes to get dressed, teeth brushed, washed, and out to morning roll call and then to breakfast. Can't waste time here at Raft. It is always, Go, Go, Go. I am hungry enough to eat hay. How about you?"

"I am never hungry at this dump," came the voice of Lester Privett. "Everything in this rat hole is garbage."

"You are just a spoiled brat, Pimple Face. You are darned lucky to get anything," retorted Bung.

Clay turned to see Arthur Diller stretching his short muscular frame.

After morning roll call and breakfast, the boys broke up into smaller groups. A few worked on the carpentry and repair crews, a few in the cannery and laundry, a few on the grounds around the buildings. The largest group was assigned to the farm detail. Many of the younger boys attended the school.

"New kid, Injun kid, follow me. You have to get your hair cut today," yelled Slopjar.

The barber, a mild appearing, frail man, looked at the Indian boy's mop of hair over the rims of his spectacles.

Clay nervously blurted out, "I don't think I get hair cut, okay?"

"I think you *will* get hair cut, you scrawny Lamanite. Okay?" said Slopjar. The mild barber added, "It won't hurt a bit, Son."

Clay reacted the only way he had learned to react under stress. He exploded into violence, thrashing and screaming, "No stupid White guy scalp me, by golly!"

The barber called on the phone for reinforcements.

. . .

The barbershop was a mess when Ted Jacobs arrived. Towels were strewn around. There was shaving cream smeared on the mirror and the barber's head. The air reeked of hair tonic from broken bottles. Slopjar and the barber were holding Clay Walker down in the barber chair.

"I got one swipe with the clippers right down the middle as you can see," said the barber. "It was like a stick of dynamite exploded in my hands."

Clay screamed at Jacobs in desperation. "Mr. Jacob, no White guy scalp my hair. I mean that."

"Will you let one of the Indian boys cut your hair?" he asked calmly.

Clay began to relax. "They be other Indian here?"

"About a dozen."

"Maybe I let Indian cut hair," Clay answered hesitantly, and then added, "but no White guy."

"Okay. I'll get one of them. No more trouble, you hear."

. . .

Ben Wallowing Bull was as big as Clay was small. He was quiet, although he was nobody's pushover. He played right tackle on the football team and was one of the school's best wrestlers.

The little Indian suspiciously sized up the big, smiling Indian. Ben spoke first.

"What's the trouble, Little Injun? Not afraid to have your hair cut are you?"

Clay avoided this topic by asking a question in return. "What you name?"

"Ben."

"Ben you only name?"

"My full name is Ben Wallowing Bull."

"Why you use funny Indian name?"

This drew a smile from Ben. "I like it."

"You be *Dineh*?"

"Yes. Down around Window Rock."

Clay relaxed and changed the subject again. "I not like *belagaana*. White Peoples no good."

Ben replied calmly, "There are bad ones and good ones."

Clay's hostility was broken. "Ben, you shave my hair. Mr. Jacob, he say I got to."

"Sure. Nothing to it."

Halfway through the haircut, Clay asked, "What a Lamanite is, Ben? Mr. Kelly, he call me Lamanite."

"That is the name the Mormons give to Indians. They are a religious group who say that the name comes from ancient history in their *Book of Mormon*. Our ancestors were among the first people who lived here. That is why we are Native Americans. Back then we were called Lamanites, after one of the early leaders."

"How you know all that, Ben?"

"I am curious and I read a lot," he smiled. "And I am a Mormon."

"I only know religion grandfather taught me," said Clay. "He say religion in sky, sun, moon, rain, trees and ancestors. I learn to chant and sing old songs."

"You are smart to have learned those ways. I wish I had learned more of our old ways."

"I not smart. Don't know to talk or write much *belagaana*."

"That doesn't make you dumb, Clay Walker. It just means that you have not had the opportunity to learn yet. They cannot speak Navajo. . . I will help you learn. Maybe later you can enroll in the school program here."

"You do that for me, Ben? You help me learn White Man language?"

"Sure. I will help you."

"We be friends, huh?" said Clay.

"You bet we will, Little Injun."

TWENTY-FOUR

At morning roll call after breakfast, Slopjar Kelly barked, "Hey Walker, Injun Kid, report to Savior Jacob's office in the Social Service Department. Looks like you get out of work today. You can cry your sad story to the bleeding hearts over there and see if they can repair your shattered life."

Defiance was still in his eyes as he presented himself at Jacob's office. The Social Worker had been around long enough to know that defiance often covered up fear.

"Clay, I want to get to know you better," he began. "I like your haircut. . . Have a chair and tell me about yourself."

The Indian boy stared sullenly at the floor.

"What do you like to do best?" Ted tried again. "You must be especially interested in something. Tell me something about your mother, the things you remember about her," he finally risked asking.

Quite unexpectedly Clay looked up into the White Man's eyes and blurted out, "Don't know what is to tell. She nothing but old damn squaw."

Jacobs waited several moments for the Indian boy to gain composure and then changed the subject. "How do you like it here by now?"

"I not like."

"I can't say as I blame you. It was a stupid question anyway. I don't particularly like it here either."

"Why you stay then?" questioned Clay.

Jacobs chuckled aloud. "That is a good question, Clay. On second thought I can't say that I don't like it altogether. I probably stay because I like the work and I like the boys. . ."

"Even me you like?" cut in Clay.

"Even you," continued Ted, smiling. "I have seen some of the boys go out of here and make something of themselves, and I kind of like to think that I had a little bit to do with it."

"What I could do?" asked Clay. "Nothing I can do here."

"There is something everyone can do well, better than anyone else. It is just a matter of looking deep enough inside them and hard enough and long enough to find it. I know how it is here," the caseworker continued. "I know some things are not as they should be. I know some of our staff are not very nice people. I know the going can get lonely and tough. When it does, you are welcome anytime to come and talk with me about it.

Jacobs changed to a more lighthearted tone. "Let's take a walk and get some air. I'll show you around some places you might not have seen yet. Okay?"

Clay nodded approval and they walked outside of the building.

Ted Jacobs never talked down to anyone. He talked with them as equals. Clay was thrilled that this adult White Man was taking time with him, the first adult other than his grandfather and uncles to address him as being worthy of consideration.

After touring the grounds and buildings, they stopped at the school. "Would you like to learn to speak and write English?" asked Ted Jacobs.

"Yeah, maybe I like that. Ben say he help me too."

"All right, let's put you in a half day of school. Let's get in the pickup. We will drive the rest of the tour."

From the pickup truck, Jacobs pointed out the lower farm, with its cow pastures, milk shed and barns, the chicken coops and egg plant. "The institution is almost self-sustaining," he explained proudly. "There stretches the upper farm, right up against the mountains." He gestured with a sweep of his hand. "There are some of the best hay fields, corn fields and fruit orchards you will find anywhere. How would you like to work on the farm?"

Since the haircut affair, Clay had become a great admirer of Ben Wallowing Bull, who had performed the task. They had become constant companions and were now known as Big Injun and Little Injun to boys and staff alike. Clay asked, "Ben, he work on farm?"

"Yes, as a matter of fact, he does."

"Then I like work there too."

"Okay, a half day in school and a half day on the farm it will be."

Clay Walker had actually enjoyed his tour of the Raft. He had to admit that he was beginning to like this White Man.

T W E N T Y - F I V E

The sun reflected off the mown hay that lay in the fields. Rusty Red sat atop the wagon, driving the matched pair of Clydesdales. His was the coveted job of every boy at the school. Clay, Bung Jackson, Arthur Diller and Ben pitched hay onto the wagon. As the morning warmed, Clay pulled off his shirt and hooked it over a post of the wagon. Rusty Red yelled down at him. "We don't take off our shirts around here. It is against the rules."

"Rule guys not around, so I take it off," replied Clay.

"Well I am around, and it is my job to report any smart guys. You are asking for trouble."

"Little Injun, you ought to do like Rusty Red told you, and put on your shirt. He will probably report you to Slopjar," said Bung Jackson.

"Okay, Bung. I make you feel better, I put on shirt," he said.

The day had slipped by rapidly. Mr. Terry, the farm supervisor's pickup was stirring up a cloud of dust down the dirt road to pick them up for evening chow.

. . .

Clay felt tired, after eating, but a pleasant tired. He just wanted to sit and do nothing special. Rusty Red, however, felt like getting everyone's attention. "Did I ever tell you guys that I am a high school graduate?" he began.

"Only about a hundred times," came a muffled voice.

Rusty Red ignored the remark. "It seems some guy spoke about the throat muscles of a salamander. I couldn't figure what that had to do with graduating, but then I could have been a little fuzzy in my hearing, as I had nipped a little Old Grandad before the ceremony. The main speaker was our town mayor, old, about eighty. He had a red face and a bald spot on the top of his head. He sure did remind me of Santa Claus without his beard. He kept talking about how this great class would be the future leaders of the country.

All the time I kept wishing he'd say, Okay, you kids, you are on your own now. Run out there and grab the bull by the tail, twist hard and make him cry uncle three times.' Then everyone could mumble an Amen and get out of that stuffy gymnasium, which by that time smelled like the boy's locker room."

"How come you are here at the Raft, Rusty Red, if you are such a smart high school guy?" cut in Bung.

"Everyone is allowed one mistake," Rusty Red replied.

Someone else picked up the challenge. "Yeah, if you are such a smart high school graduate, what do you want to be when you grow up?"

"He doesn't want to grow up," said another. "He wants to be Peter Pan."

Why did a person have to *be* something anyway, thought Clay. He took off his clothes and crawled into bed, facing the wall.

"I will tell you what I would really like to be," continued the redhead. "I would like to be the guy that holds the red flag when they are building a road. This guy just sits there holding this red flag and telling the people in the cars when they can go. You never have to talk to anybody, maybe just say thanks once in awhile."

"That ought to be some sight," mumbled someone. "A redhead holding a red flag, getting a red sunburn."

"What about the little Injun back in the corner," someone yelled. "What does he want to be?"

"Bet he wants to be a chief on the reservation."

"I'll guess he wants to be a movie actor, the Indian who always says `How' and `Ugh.'"

"Yeah, Little Injun," said Rusty Red. "What do you want to be when you grow up?"

Clay rolled over and sat up in his bed, anger flushing his face. "Would like to be warrior so could scalp you."

"Well now, listen to that. He speaks with straight tongue."

"Okay, knock it off! That is enough," came a soft, but authoritative voice, as Big Injun stood up slowly and faced the group. He gave Rusty Red a challenging stare and the laughter and loud talking ceased.

Just then, Slopjar Kelley entered the door. "Speaking of the redskin in the corner," he said, "he is also a smart alleck who won't wear his shirt on work detail. That is breaking a rule. Crawl out, Redskin. There will be no sack time for you on this night. I have some nice dirty floors for you to scrub in the downstairs area. You will scrub them on hands and knees with soap, water, bucket and scrub brush, until they are bleached white to my satisfaction. If you are lucky, you may just finish in time to get some leftover breakfast.

Clay hurt under the humiliation. He pulled on his pants and shirt and felt all eyes turned in his direction. As he left the sleeping quarters he gave Rusty Red a cold stare.

T W E N T Y - S I X

Clay pulled back on the reins and climbed off the seat of the flat-bed wagon shouting excitedly at Ben, who was lofting a pitchfork of hay on top of another wagon load. "Hey, Ben, you see me drive team?"

"Let's sit down and take in some of that shade, Little Partner," Ben yelled back. "It is really a hot one today."

Clay was so excited he couldn't contain himself. "You see me, Ben?" he repeated. "You see me just now drive them horses by myself? Mr. Terry, when he see me do it, say I can always drive them. He gave Rusty Red different job and he plenty mad."

"You bet I saw you," replied Ben. "It looked like you were doing a great job. Don't worry about that redhead either. Let's try to treat him kind. I have a hunch that he is not all that bad."

"That plenty good of Mr. Terry to give me respon. . . respons. . ."

"Responsibility," assisted Ben.

"Yeah, to let me drive them team by myself."

"I guess he just figures that you are the best one for the job, Little Injun."

"Ben, that very best thing happen me here at Raft. No one before trust me to do something like that."

"You are a good buddy, Little Injun. It is good to hear you talk. We are a lot alike. I understand how you feel. You are coming along with your language lessons too.

"You know in lots of ways we have it over those city kids. Have they slept out at night and watched the moon rise over the crest of a mountain? Could they enjoy the smell of yucca, mesquite and sage, or the beauty of ocotillo after rain? Have they ever seen a coyote on a hill against a night sky?"

Clay nodded agreement, understanding the things of which Ben spoke. They slipped into silence and gazed over the valley, clear out to the Great Salt Lake reflecting the sun like a mirror.

Ben spoke again after some time. "And you know we haven't got it bad. As tough as the Raft may seem at times, it is a home for us, Clay. . . You see that team of Clydesdales you were driving. You might feel sorry for them having to work so hard. But they love it. I'll have to show you all of their ribbons and trophies they have won. They pull together. That is their secret. They don't have it so bad. They get curried down each evening, get fed good and get clean straw to sleep on. Little Injun, for a couple of misfits we got it pretty good too."

"Never had friend like you, Ben."

"I have to start thinking about living on the outside. I am older than many of you and my release time is nearing," said Ben Wallowing Bull seriously.

"I never think of when we got to split up, Big Injun." "You will do just fine if you always keep learning. . . Here comes Mr. Terry in the truck to take us to chow. Are you as hungry as I am?"

"Sure am, Ben. I always hungry."

it. Everyone knew the redhead was out to get him ever since Little Injun got his job driving the team."

"That's right, Mr. Ellsworth," chimed in Bung. "Anyone would have fought Rusty Red with his big mouth. Little Injun tried his best to prevent it, because he made a promise to Mr. Jacobs to stay out of trouble."

Clay looked astonished that these two had spoken in his behalf. Maybe he did have friends.

"Okay, Little Injun, I believe what your friends say," said Mr. Ellsworth, stifling a grin. "But you, Rusty Red, being as you like to be in the coops so much, can clean them for the next two weeks. It is getting light so both of you get showered up for breakfast. You smell like. . .well, like chicken shit. Hurry up now and we will say no more about this incident."

TWENTY-EIGHT

Clay Walker was rubbing his eye later in the day when he ran into Ben Wallowing Bull. Although he had taken a beating, he still felt that the skinny redhead was not really a bad fellow underneath, if he could just get to know him better.

When Ben saw Clay's eye, he asked casually, "Where did you get the shiner?"

"What is shiner you talk about?"

"Your black eye that is puffing out like a frog's eye."

"Oh that. Not like to say about it, Ben."

"There is no need to cover up for that redhead. It is impossible to keep secrets here at the Raft. I think that I am about to have a word or two with the redhead myself. . ."

"Don't want you fight my battles, Big Injun."

"I am doing this for myself. I should have done it a long time ago."

"Wish you not do, Ben. He think I tell you. I want to be his friend."

"I know that I told you we should try to be friends with him; but his bullying has got to stop."

The showdown came just before lights-out. Big Injun walked to the center of the floor and announced in a loud voice, "I understand there is a big-mouthed redhead who likes to beat up guys half his size."

Bedtime chatter ceased. All eyes turned toward Rusty Red, who was sitting on his bed. He knew that he couldn't back down with all eyes upon him. He stood up and accepted the challenge. "I don't like some of your description of me, Injun."

"That is mighty tough, because I have got some more. I think you are a bully, all hot air and mouth, and I intend to clean your plow."

"You and how many more of your tribe? I can see that your little Injun friend has run to his big tough friend for help again."

"Not so. Let's get it straight," said Ben. "Little Injun did not squeal on you. I heard it from almost everyone here, except him. For some strange reason, he wanted to protect you."

Rusty Red looked over at Clay with a puzzled expression.

"Let's get on with it," continued Ben. "Let's see how tough you are now with everyone watching."

Rusty Red's fist shot out at Big Injun's head, but Ben ducked under the wild swing and brought his fist out straight from the shoulder into the redhead's nose. Blood spurted from the nose as he flew off his feet. His eyes rolled back in his head and he fell back unconscious. The fight was over quicker than it took to get it started.

"Throw some water on him," someone yelled.

"Here comes Slopjar."

"Kill the lights!"

"Get the redhead in bed. Keep him quiet. He's coming around now."

It was silent when Slopjar looked into the barracks. It continued quiet for several minutes after he left. Then a groggy voice spoke from the darkness.

"This is Rusty Red making an announcement. This is Big-Mouthed Rusty Red with a broken nose. I want to apologize to Little Injun and I want to say that Big Injun whipped me like I deserved. I hope we are all still friends. Now I would like very much to put my throbbing nose to rest, so Amen."

"Apologies accepted. No hard feelings," said Big Injun.

"Me too," echoed Little Injun. "You bet we be friends, Rusty Red."

A hardy laugh from everyone shattered the darkness and eased the tension.

After several moments silence, Ben slipped out of his bunk and knelt by Clay's. "I have been doing some thinking, Little Injun. I owe you an apology too. Here I have been telling you we should love our fellow men and be friends with Rusty Red and I end up being a hypocrite by fighting as a way of solving things. I apologize for my behavior."

"It all come out okay, Ben. Rusty Red, he now our friend. Maybe little fight be need to get us together sometime."

Ben chuckled softly. "Maybe you are right, Clay. . . Goodnight."

"Goodnight, Big Injun."

TWENTY-NINE

Ernest Harlington Kelly had been called Chubby, Fatso or Piggy ever since he could remember. Now it was Slopjar. In fact, none of the boys had ever heard his real name. To his face, it was Sir or Mr. Kelly. All other times it was Slopjar. He would show them all some day. But he never did. The best he could do was work as the underpaid supervisor of Group A of the State Industrial School. . .the Raft.

Through his job he could use his resentment on juveniles placed in his charge. His verbal and physical abuse of them became greater each day as his sadism surfaced. This particular day he seemed unusually mean as he called roll, prior to marching them to the mess hall.

Roll call went routinely with, "Here, Sir. Here, Sir," barked off in cadence until the name Arthur Diller. . .and silence. Bung Jackson always answered for the deaf mute Arthur. Slopjar growled a second time, "Arthur Diller."

Again there was no answer. "Bung Jackson, you stupid jerk, don't you always answer for the dummy?"

"Yes, Sir," stammered Bung. "But I don't know where Arthur is, Sir."

Slopjar noted this on his roll, then continued. Upon reaching the name of Lester Privett there was silence once again. "All right, little brats, it seems that there is some hanky panky going on. If that is the way you want to play, well I can play too. There will be no chow until our two missing links show up. Now turn about face and march your bodies right back into the barracks."

When they were back inside, Slopjar addressed them again. "Now," he said sarcastically, "does anyone just happen to know where Mr. Privett and Mr. Diller might be? Rusty Red, any grapevine chatter or rumors among the brats?"

"No, Sir, Mr. Kelly. Not a thing," he lied.

Suddenly Slopjar's expression changed. "Ah-hah, I believe I have received enlightenment, and if I am right there will be misery to pay."

He started up the stairs to the sleeping quarters on the second floor. Some of the boys followed, Little Injun among them. Slopjar pushed open the door with a bang. At the far end of bunk beds, a pale face with wide eyes peered out from under a blanket, and across the isle lay Arthur Diller.

Slopjar Kelly began to move down the aisle. Arthur jumped quickly off his bed and stood at attention. Lester's eyes grew wider.

Slopjar stopped by the bed, looking down at the frightened face. "Well, well, it seems my hunch was right. A little goofing off taking place in the middle of the day."

"No, Sir, Mr. Kelly. Honest. We weren't goofing off. I felt sick and Arthur felt that he ought to stay to look after me. It wasn't Arthur's fault at all."

"A likely story." He turned to Rusty Red, who was standing to the side. "Redhead, get the *Big Hand*. I intend to make this sniffling brat wish he *was* sick."

Rusty Red stood frozen, refusing to move.

"All right, I'll get it myself," fumed Slopjar. "It is time you were replaced anyway, Redhead."

He waddled toward the wall where the dreaded *Big Hand* hung from a hook. Arthur Diller started flapping his arms and making squawking sounds. "Shut up, you stupid mute," Slopjar shouted, as he walked back to Lester's bed with the *Big Hand*.

The *Big Hand* was made out of one inch plywood, and was attached to the end of a long handle so it formed a paddle. Small nails were driven through the hand so they protruded on the other side of the board about one-sixteenth of an inch.

"Get out of that sack you sickly brat or I'll drag you out by the hair of your head," he snarled.

Lester crawled meekly out from beneath the blanket, trying to hide his naked white body.

"Bend over that bottom bunk, Pimple Face," commanded Kelly. "The rest of you watch very closely."

Lester began to whimper and then to plead. "Please, Sir, Mr. Kelly. I promise it will never happen again. I can't take pain."

"You should have thought of that before, Pimple Face. Bend over!"

Lester obeyed, his body quivering. The Big Hand came down on his buttocks with a smack. A dozen or more tiny puncture wounds penetrated the skin and blood bubbles appeared. Lester screamed in pain.

Arthur Diller, who had been flapping his arms helplessly, exploded in a burst of rage. His powerful body lunged forward on Slopjar, knocking him off balance and into the side of the bunk bed. Arthur's strong hands grasped the fat neck and began to squeeze. The fat face went redder as the hands squeezed tighter. Just as Slopjar looked as if he was going to black-out, he freed his hand that was holding the heavy wooden paddle. He raised it and brought it down sideways at the base of Arthur's skull. He slumped to the floor unconscious.

Clay Walker, rushed at Slopjar Kelly, jumping onto his back, clawing and swinging his fists and arms. The huge fat man backhanded him once and sent him sailing across the room.

Breathing heavily, Slopjar gradually gained his composure and rubbed his neck for several moments before he could speak. "Now is there anyone else who cares to dissent?" he gasped.

Silence greeted his question.

"All right," said Slopjar. "I shall proceed with the punishment."

Nine more times the Big Hand raised and fell. The pale boy finally slipped to the floor unconscious, his flesh like raw hamburger.

Slopjar Kelly wiped the sweat from his forehead. He walked across the room and hung the *Big Hand* back on the wall. "The rest of you clean up these two and be out front in ten minutes. We are late for chow."

No one felt much like eating. There was quiet murmuring throughout the day and at night when lights went out.

THIRTY

The first thing that caught Clay's attention as he blinked his eyes against the dawn, was the feet dangling a few inches off the floor. Then came Lester's whimpering and Bung's frantic chatter.

"Oh Lordy! Wake up! Everyone wake up. It is awful terrible. Poor Arthur has hung himself. Arthur is deader than dead."

Arthur Diller's body was swaying gently back and forth only inches off the floor. His belt was cinched tightly around his neck and the buckle was hooked over a prong of the metal protector that covered the light.

"Let's get him down," someone yelled. Others began scrambling from their beds as the tragedy became a reality to them.

Bung and Clay and a couple of other boys grabbed hold of Arthur's body, and as soon as they did, the metal fixture pulled from the ceiling. The lifeless form fell heavily to the floor, followed by a shower of plaster.

The boys stood around staring at Arthur's *body*. He was no longer a person. Just a *body*. Lester Pimple Face kept crying. Clay sat down on a bottom bunk, totally drained of energy. He was terrified of the dead. His Navajo background taught that death was sacred and certain rituals had to be performed so that the *chindi*, or ghost of the dead one did not linger and become angry with the living for not preparing it for its death journey. Bung Jackson eased down beside him on the bunk. "In his case it was best, huh, Clay Walker? He couldn't talk, couldn't hear. He is better off dead, huh Little Injun?"

"Don't know, Bung. . . Dead is nothing. Alive is everything."

That night, in silence, alone, Clay sang softly, mostly to himself, although other boys listened in silent respect. He sang an old song his grandfather had taught him. He sang of beauty, not of death.

THIRTY-ONE

The whispering was much like any other night shortly after lights-out. But it kept on and rose in volume until someone would quiet it with a sudden, "Ssshhhh!"

"Has everyone that's going got their clothes on? It's quite a drop to the ground. Be careful."

Shadowy figures started jumping out the window. Then the unplanned happened. "Ohhh, I hurt my foot," came a cry of pain.

"Run! Slopjar is coming. Everyone for himself."

Phantom figures scattered in all directions. Lights began to pop on all over the campus.

. . .

The inside of the barn was dark. Clay Walker couldn't make out forms or images. His hand searched out for Takawashi Kami, the Japanese boy, who had been sleeping beside him in the hay loft. All he felt was cold wood with cracks and splinters. During the run the two of them had become separated from the others and had luckily found shelter in an old barn.

Clay lifted himself up on one elbow. The cold crept in under the dusty burlap sack he had thrown over himself for a blanket. His neck was stiff from being propped up on the leather horse collar he had used for a pillow.

"Tak," he whispered. And then louder. "Tak, where are you?" He found the ladder down from the hay loft. He could see night through the barn door and headed toward it. The moon was full. It was a see-your-breath night. "Hey Tak, that you?"

"Yeah, it's me."

"What is matter with you? Golly, Tak, you crazy, out here walk around in middle of night."

"I just couldn't sleep in that barn. I had to keep warm some way."

"Tak, we going to walk all night and get no place?" Clay asked after awhile.

"I guess so. I sure can't sleep. Have you got any better ideas?"

"Yeah, maybe I got one. Why we not walk and get someplace instead of walk back and forward. Okay?"

"Okay, Little Injun, you are right."

As they trudged through the night, Clay started to talk. "I not trust peoples too much, except Big Injun. Now I finding that you not a bad fellow. How come you get sent to Raft, Tak? You seem like guy who not have trouble."

"I keep telling myself that same thing, Little Injun. I am not like all the others at the Raft."

Clay asked again, "What you do to be sent to Raft, Tak? Thought Japanese not supposed to get trouble or it disgrace ancestors and tribe people. That right, what I hear?"

"You heard right, and this Jap kid has sadly disgraced his honorable ancestors many times. It is really not so different between me and you as it seems," said Takawashi Kami. "My Papasan and Mamasan have always been too busy making moneysan, so I thought I would make them notice me. I am feeling sorry for myself, huh?"

"I sure am interest about you, Tak. You got problem too, huh?"

"Boy, you know I got problems."

"But what you *do* to be so bad, Tak?"

"I wasn't going to tell you because I am ashamed. . .I am a firebug. . ."

"What is firebug, Tak? I pretty dumb about things."

"It is someone who lights fires. . .just to watch them burn. . .like garages, sheds, warehouses, things like that. The fifty-cent term for a firebug, is pyromaniac. I am supposed to be sick, up here in my mind. Actually, though, I'm not. I am ashamed. I almost wish I hadn't run now."

"Me too, Tak. We really mess things up, huh. Bet Mr. Jacob think I no good now. . .Bet Ben be ashamed of me too. Wonder where other guys are? Sure wish we not get lost from them."

"Me too. I wish I was back at the Raft."

"No kidding, Tak? You wish you back there?"

"Yeah. It wasn't too bad a place except for a few like Slopjar Kelly."

"You think we maybe should go back, Tak?"

"I don't know, Little Injun. They will put us in the Buckets for awhile. . ."

"What are Buckets, Tak?"

"The Buckets are solitary confinement. They put you in a cell all by yourself, just a wood slab for a bed, a toilet and a sink, a small high window with bars, and a dim light bulb. You got nothing to do, but think."

"Tak, let's give up to Police, huh."

"Okay, Little Injun. Let's do it."

Many days later, after hitching several rides and spending several cold nights in ditches and barns, they saw the sign as daylight came: WELCOME TO BEAVER CITY—elevation 1238—population 879. Two tired and hungry boys turned themselves in—two hundred miles away from the RAFT. They had become close friends.

THIRTY-TWO

The bad news was that they spent time in the buckets as Tak said they would. The good news was that Slopjar Kelly had been fired from his job and was in police custody charged with assault. Then another crises came for Clay Walker. Big Injun was leaving, being released from the Raft. The news spread to all the boys. Little Injun ran all the way from the lower farm to Ted Jacob's office.

"I am sorry, Mr. Jacobs, but got to see you now," he gasped, still breathing heavily from his run.

"Come in. Sit down; you look pretty tired."

Clay blurted out his question. "Mr. Jacobs, is true Big Injun leaving the Raft?"

"Yes, it is true."

"Think I better go with him."

"No, your time will come later. Remember that Ben came before you did and he is older."

"But what I going do without Big Injun? He is best friend I have."

"You can make other friends. You can't live with him forever. And Ben will write to you. It will be good practice for your reading and writing."

"It not same," he muttered as he left.

That night, Little Injun and Big Injun lay in their beds and talked long after lights-out. Ben had moved into Arthur Diller's bed to be closer to his friend.

"What I going to do after you gone, Ben?"

"You will make it just fine, Little Injun. And I will write to you."

"Mr. Jacobs say same thing."

"He is right in a lot of things."

"I know that, Ben. He is best White guy I know, but just not same as me and you."

"Clay, my friend, you have got to stop thinking of people as White or Indian. Can't you just think of them as people? Tak is not *Dineh* and not White, and he is our friend."

"Is true you try to be warrior in Army, Ben?"

"Maybe. I might beat you to being a warrior, huh? There is a war going on in Europe and it looks like the United States is going to get into it. I am thinking of joining the Marine Corps. They are the best warriors, I hear."

"I bet you make good Marine, Big Injun."

.   .   .

The day of Ben Wallowing Bull's departure was particularly sad because Big Injun had been such a stabilizing influence in the *Group*. Ben was dressed in his best clothes and his hair was neatly combed. His easy-going smile and calm voice had eased many tense situations at the school.

Clay Walker looked like a lost waif, standing in the crowd, not knowing what to do. Just as Ben Wallowing Bull was about to climb into the car that would take him away, Clay rushed forth and grabbed him in a bear hug. All his pent-up feelings burst forth in one big sob, as tears flowed down his cheeks. Then he turned and ran quickly into the building. The team of Big Injun, Little Injun parted.

THIRTY-THREE

Clay Walker was moody for days after Ben Wallowing Bull's departure. Then, as quickly as he had withdrawn, he came out of his shell and announced to Ted Jacobs, "By golly, I have whip tough problem. I going to make it okay like Ben say."

This time he stuck to his commitment. He took care of his farm chores early in the morning and requested full day schooling. He struggled with spelling, reading, writing. But his desire to learn increased even more by an exciting event that started happening in his life: Mail Call. News that a special letter was waiting, sent him speeding toward the Social Worker's office. "You got a letter for me, Mr. Jacobs?"

"Matter of fact I have."

"Big Injun, I got letter from Ben, huh?"

Ted handed him the letter.

Clay stared at the envelope like it was something sacred. "Ben write me letter just like he say he would." Then he looked up at Ted Jacobs. "I never had letter before."

Awkwardly Clay started fumbling with the flap, being careful not to tear it, taking out the paper inside. He stared at it in silence and handed it to Ted. "Mr. Jacobs, maybe you read my first letter to me. I am learning, but not good enough to make sure I read it correct."

"Sure, I'll be glad to read it for you."

To my friend, Little Injun,

I am sorry I haven't written sooner, but I am in the Marines and kept pretty busy. My parole was lifted early and I joined up right away. Boot Camp is the name for our training, where we learn to be real warriors. The Marines are the best. Looks like I beat you to being a warrior, but work hard and study, and maybe soon you can join me.

The training and discipline I received in the Raft has really helped me. There are a couple of other *Dineh* in our company and they are having tough times. They still go by Indian time and it gets them into trouble. So, be glad you are at the Raft. You are used to getting up early, making your bed, washing pots and pans, which we call KP.

This Marine Corps is the greatest, Clay. It gives a redskin like me a chance to be equal to everyone else. In the Corps they judge each of us by our performance. My D.I. (that stands for drill instructor) is a Negro. He has been in combat in Europe and was wounded, so is here as an instructor for awhile. My squad leader is a Mexican. It reminds me of our group at the Raft.

I am learning about many different types of weapons—how to use them, clean them, take them apart and put them together again. We have races to see who can do it fastest.

Besides learning these military things, I am learning to respect myself. I am learning to rely more on myself and to walk proud like your grandfather said. You can do the same. Listen to Mr. Jacobs. Learn everything you can.

One thing I know Clay, is that there *is* a Great Mystery, a someone in charge, a Heavenly Father. We are all His children and are loved, and must try our best as we walk the earth.

Well, Little Injun, I will say goodbye for now. You better learn quick to write. I want some letters at Mail Call. When you write, tell me all the news from the Raft, and how all the guys are doing.

Your friend,
Big Injun (Ben)

Ted Jacobs handed the letter back to Clay. He folded it and put it back into his shirt pocket. This letter did the trick. Clay began to study and learn in unbelievable strides. He became an excellent student overnight. It was one of his proudest moments when he answered one of Ben's letters in his own writing without the help of anyone.

THIRTY-FOUR

Winter. Snow covered the world. It seemed to purify it, giving it a fresh start and each individual a new chance. Only one cloud hung dark over the season. The United States had declared war because a place called Pearl Harbor had been bombed. It was a far away place that none of the boys had heard of before, so they seemed unconcerned, although the staff seemed affected by news of the war.

Winter turned to spring and spring was blending into the hot days of summer. They were all unexpectantly summoned to the gymnasium. It was Saturday when they got to take care of personal needs, so there was grumbling heard.

When Clay entered the gym he heard the buzz of excitement. A table was set in the middle of the gym floor. A man in a uniform was seated at the table. His pants were blue with red stripes down the legs. His jacket was blue with shiny brass buttons. On the arms were several pointed stripes. On the table lay his white cap and white gloves.

Everyone was soon in the gym. The man in uniform stood and the talking stopped. "I am Sergeant Rayburn of the United States Marine Corps," he began. "I am here to offer some of you a way out of here."

There was cheering. The Sergeant smiled and then held up his hands for quiet.

"Wait until you hear my proposition and you may not be so eager to get out of here. It might be like jumping from the frying pan into the fire. As I said, I am a member of the United States Marine Corps. . ."

Clay's hand shot up and the Sergeant acknowledged him. "Is it true they are the best warriors?" he asked.

There was laughter.

"You better believe it," said Sergeant Rayburn. "The Marines are the very best warriors the military has. . . Now hold the rest of your questions until I finish.

"I am sure by now that you are aware that the United States is at war. The Japanese made a surprise attack on Pearl Harbor last December seventh.

Everyone stared at Takawashi Kami. Tak stared at the floor.

"You may not know what Pearl Harbor is or what it represents to us. Pearl Harbor is in the Hawaiian Islands. It is the port for most of our naval warships of the Pacific fleet. It is possession of the United States. The Japs wiped out most of our fleet. Hundreds of our men went down with their ships. President Roosevelt has declared war against Japan. Gentlemen, we need all of the warriors we can get." He smiled toward Clay.

Everyone kept sneaking looks at Tak. He was now the enemy. Clay felt sorry for him. Tak was not one of *those* Japs. Enemy was a vague bunch of people far away. Tak was here. Takawashi Kami was friend.

"I am here today," continued the Sergeant, "to ask for volunteers. But before you volunteer, let me tell you that it will be very tough. You will eventually be sent to combat and some of you will be killed or wounded in action. You will have to go through eight to sixteen weeks of intensive physical hardship, weapons, tactics, and military procedure, depending upon the type of unit you are assigned, and the need for replacements on the battle fronts. And I must emphasize to you again. . . The reality is that some of you will be killed or wounded fighting the enemy."

He let these last words sink in for several seconds amid total silence.

"Some of you may not qualify or meet our standards, but we will give you all the opportunity. I can take those of you eighteen or older, seventeen in special circumstances, with guardian consent. Are there any volunteers? Who wants to be a United States Marine?"

Slowly, Clay Walker felt his hand raising.

. . .

But it was not all that easy to get into the United States Marine Corps. Clay Walker was perhaps seventeen, maybe even sixteen, and looked much younger. Who was to prove his age? He needed an okay from one of his uncles. His telegram, his letters went unanswered week after week. The Indian Agent was unable to locate them. Time hung like a huge piece of sandstone around his neck.

Clay was about to fall into despair when a telegram arrived. It said simply:

> Clay Walker can be a warrior in the Marines. He will be a
> good one. I his uncle who knows him best say so.
>
> —Happy Jack.

The telegram was quickly forwarded to the Marine recruiter.

Clay Walker's parting with his Social Worker, Ted Jacobs was tearful. It was his last tie to an adult friend. Finally he broke away and turned his back on the Raft forever. *Walks Two Worlds* walked once again into the unknown.

BOOK THREE
WARRIOR

THIRTY-FIVE

The new recruits stood in line waiting for their haircuts. They had been sworn in. Clay Walker—*Walks Two Worlds*—was going to be a warrior in the United States Marine Corps.

"Sure doesn't take long," said the chubby blond boy in front of him. "My blond curls that took two months to grow will be gone in thirty seconds."

"It won't hurt a bit," said Clay, laughing.

"What's so funny about losing your hair?"

"I was just thinking of my first White Man haircut ever. My hair was five times as long as yours. . . Hung down below my shoulders. I tore that barbershop apart. I thought the White guy was going to scalp me."

The blond boy laughed with him now. "You an Indian?" he asked.

"Yeah. Navajo."

Next, they received their gear: uniforms, duffel bag, toilet kit, blankets. They were assigned barracks and bunk beds and were ready to turn in when taps sounded.

Reveille was new to most of them and always came too early. After chow they received their steel helmets and rifles. Their first training sessions involved their rifles.

The drill instructor, Sergeant Ochoa, was a small, compact built man. He held a rifle up. "This is an M-1 rifle, the best there is in the world at the present time. It is a semi-automatic weapon, which means that it fires each time the trigger is pulled. It carries a clip of eight rounds. This weapon will become your best friend. It will become your third arm. You will keep it cleaner than your toothbrush. You will learn to field strip it, break it down and put it together in the dark, in under a minute."

Clay smiled as he remembered Big Injun telling him this in one of his letters. At the first rifle inspection, the D.I. stopped in front of Private Clay Walker. "Are you sure you are old enough to be in the Marines, Private?"

"Yes, Sir."

"How old are you? You look about fourteen and four feet tall. I thought I was small."

"I am five foot two, one hundred and twenty-five pounds and seventeen years old, I believe, Sir," said Clay, looking straight into the drill instructor's eyes. Looking into someone's eyes had always been difficult for him, due to his Navajo culture.

"What do you mean, you *think* you are seventeen? Don't you know?"

"No, Sir. I was born on a reservation where there weren't many records. But my uncle says I am old enough. He signed for me."

The D.I. snapped the rifle out of Clay's hands, pulled open the breach and looked down the barrel. "You keep a clean rifle, Private. That is a mark in your favor. But you sure are a little one. Do you think you can become a real Marine?"

"Yes Sir, I know I can," answered Clay.

"We will see. We will see. . ."

.   .   .

At a night training session the recruits were asked to identify sounds in the dark. A faint click brought an answer from Private Clay Walker. "That was the safety being released on an M-1 rifle."

"That is correct, Private Walker. You may just make a Marine after all," commended the D.I. "The rest of you better learn that sound fast or you could be dead."

Day after day the recruits went through the process of learning weapons, tactics, discipline, military procedure, physical conditioning--learning to be marines, modern warriors. But they were not yet full fledged warriors; they had yet to be proven in battle.

Clay achieved expert in firing the M-1 rifle and the M-2 carbine, and a marksman's medal in the .45 pistol. He also earned the right for his first weekend pass.

THIRTY-SIX

"I don't think I want to go to the city," said Private Clay Walker.

"Come on, go with us. You will love it. We have worked our rear ends off and we deserve it." This was a big, gangly, Nebraska farmer, Clay knew only as Gooch.

"I only been to a big city a couple of times. I don't like big cities. There are too many people. . .too crowded with buildings and lots of noise," said Clay.

"You will love San Diego," said a Private Foote, from Los Angeles. He was muscular, suntanned, a native Californian. "I know this area. It is a military man's delight. Lots of fun, things to do, great night life. You can't vegetate here on base."

"Yep. It is settled. You are going with us, Walker," agreed Gooch. "We will show you a good time. Foote tells me there is a great drinking place called *The Blue Light*. Lots of girls, too."

"I don't drink whiskey or beer," answered Clay.

"You can eat pretzels and hard boiled eggs then," insisted Foote. "Come on, get in your dress duds and let's go."

Reluctantly, Clay agreed under the pressure from his buddies.

San Diego was a beautiful city. The weather was balmy, with a breeze blowing in from the sea. They visited Balboa Park, strolled on the beach, hiked up to Cabrillo monument, commanding a view everywhere around. The city spread out like jewels in the sun. The Pacific Ocean was lined with warships of all kinds. They stopped for hamburgers and milk shakes.

"You were right; this is fun," admitted Clay.

"The best is yet to come," said Foote, with a wink at Gooch. "Wait until we get to *The Blue Light*. Let's head back and get there before it gets too crowded."

San Diego was even prettier at night, with colored lights everywhere. Clay's eyes took it all in with amazement at what men had built.

The Blue Light was already crowded with servicemen in Army, Navy, and Marine uniforms. It was a rectangular building with a long bar where men were sitting on stools drinking and laughing. Round tables and chairs were spread throughout the rest of the floor, with a postage stamp size dance floor and a nickelodeon blaring out jazz music. Dim blue lights were on the walls. Scantily clad girls were rushing around serving drinks. Others stood talking to GIs at the bar.

"Why is it so dark in here?" asked Clay.

"It adds to the atmosphere, makes it romantic," said Gooch, winking again at Foote.

"Although this is called *The Blue Light*, it is really a red light, said Foote.

"I don't think I like it here. I will meet you later," said Clay, getting up from the table where a girl in a brief outfit had seated them.

"No," said Foote, easing him back down in his chair. "Remember how you enjoyed the rest of the day. Give this a chance."

A waitress was at their table.

"A beer for me and the Gooch," ordered Foote. "And a seven-up for our buddy here. That okay, Walker?"

"Yeah, that is okay."

Clay's eyes were getting accustomed to the dimness of the smoke filled, noisy room. His eyes stopped on a scantily clad young lady with black hair, talking to a GI at the bar. Something seemed familiar about her. Then a stunning recognition hit him. "Rose! Rose Yazzie!" he shouted above the din of the room. He stood up so abruptly that he knocked over his chair. "Rose-My-Only-Daughter," he shouted again, as he fought his way through the crowd.

The girl turned around in surprise. She recognized him and was shocked, then embarrassed, then horrified. She tried to leave but it was too late.

"Rose, what a surprise!"

He tired to hug her, and awkwardly she let him, pushing him gently but quickly away. She looked around self-consciously.

"Clay Walker. What a surprise seeing you in the *belagaana* world," she said, trying to put enthusiasm into her voice. "It has been such a long time. I hardly know you."

"Yes, it has been a long time. Much water has run under the bridge, as White Men say."

"Clay Walker, a United States Marine. How handsome you are in your uniform. . ."

"What are you doing here, Rose?" he asked.

Hesitantly she groped for words. "I. . . I work here. . . Remember I told you that I would be coming back to this world. . ."

"You work *here*?" he asked. "What is it that you do?"

"I serve people. . . I entertain. . ."

"How do you do this entertain? What do you do?" he asked again.

The GI that Rose had been talking with tapped him on the shoulder. "She entertains guys like me who have money, Shorty. Now shove off."

"This is true, Rose?"

"Please, Clay. You better leave. I am sorry that you had to learn of me. Please don't get me fired. I need the money. I make lots of money here. . ."

"Money? Money? What good is money for what you do?"

They stared at each other, tears forming in Rose's eyes. The past, the many years drifted between them.

"I said shove off, Shorty," the GI said, growing impatient. "I have money that says Rose entertains me." He grabbed Rose's arm. "Let's go upstairs and ditch this clod," he said, shoving Clay against the bar.

Something exploded inside of Clay's mind. His fist shot out and caught the GI in the nose, knocking him sliding on his rear. Chairs went tumbling. A table tipped over. Chaos exploded, as Clay's buddies came slugging their way to his aid. Other GIs joined on each side, not caring which side, just enjoying the action. Bottles shattered, drinks sloshed over. Someone shouted a warning. "MPs are coming. Shore Patrol. Let's get out of here."

Two burly MPs came at Clay. He punched one in the stomach and he went down gasping for air. Clay was swinging, kicking, yelling. Three more MPs arrived and finally subdued him enough to handcuff him. As he was being dragged outside, he heard Rose shouting at him. "I am sorry Clay. I am sorry."

The Paddy Wagon pulled right up to the door. There were a dozen or more MPs and Shore Patrol trying to restore order. They handcuffed six GIs and a couple of navy swabs.

"We will have to get another Paddy Wagon. Call for more assistance," ordered the MP in charge. "Put them all in the stockade. Maybe a week or so will cool them off."

The siren went on as the Military Police van moved out. Clay looked around at the sorry bunch with him in the Paddy Wagon. There was Gooch with a puffed lip and Foote with two swollen eyes.

"I am sure sorry, guys. I sure messed up your plans, huh?"

"Man, you really went wild," said Gooch. "But what the heck. . . It was some good action. Probably was more fun than what we had planned anyway."

"Did you know that broad. . .er woman?" asked Foote. "You acted like you were her long lost jealous lover."

Clay looked at the floor. "She was my friend. . .a long time ago," he said.

THIRTY-SEVEN

The military policeman entered the stockade and yelled down the cell block. "Walker, Private Clay Walker."

"Down here," came the reply.

The MP walked down the corridor, jangled some keys and opened the cell door. "You are lucky, Private Walker. You get out of the stockade early. Someone important wants to see you at the BOQ Rec Room."

"Bachelor Officer Quarters. Wow! Big deal, huh. Must really be important."

"Seems to be. Lots of security and secret stuff. You have five minutes to get yourself cleaned up. I am instructed to escort you there."

There were MPs all around the building when Clay was deposited at the door to the BOQ Recreation Room. The one at the door checked Clay's ID and looked at a list on his clipboard. "Private Clay Walker." He double checked Clay's military service number. "Okay, Private Walker, you are cleared to go in."

When Clay entered the room, he was surprised to see about forty other Navajo Marines in the room. He took a seat by a Tsosie boy he recognized. "What goes here?" he asked.

"You got me. Looks like a Navajo pow wow. It is all a big secret."

The hum of voices stopped as an older Marine with graying hair, stood up and walked to the center of the room.

"You are all wondering why all of these Navajo faces are here together and why this council was called."

There was laughter as some of the tension was eased.

"I am here to tell you why. First let me introduce myself. I am staff Sergeant Philip Johnston. I am rather old to be a Sergeant and even to be in the Marines. I served my time in World War I. I received permission to re-enter the military to direct a program which will involve you gentlemen here today.

First I must caution you that everything said in this room must remain here. You are to discuss it with no one. Our program will be classified *Top Secret*."

This got everyone's attention.

"You see standing before you an aging *belagaana*," continued Sergeant Philip Johnston, getting their further attention. "But in my heart, I am *Dineh*. I am Navajo like you down inside. I speak your native tongue as good or better than most of you. I have been to more nightway chants, blessing ways and other sings than most of you put together. I know many of your parents and grandparents. I know your food, your customs, your traditions. I am more Navajo than White. I am one of you. So listen to me!"

He switched into Navajo, giving them an old Navajo greeting. Then he continued in English.

"I was raised in *Dinetah*. I grew up on the reservation. My parents were missionaries among you. Many of you have seen me upon that land."

Some heads nodded in recognition.

"There are some of you here from Ft. Wingate, Ganado, Two Grey Hills, Shiprock, Ft. Defiance and many other places in *Dinetah*. I see many clans represented here: The Rabbit People, The Mud People, The Red House People, the Salt Water People, The Near Mountain People. . ."

He paused to take a sip of water.

"Now that you know I am no stranger to the *Dineh*, let us get down to the business of why we are here. The Japanese, have broken every code our intelligence people have devised. They learn of our troop and ship deployment almost as soon as our orders are relayed. They are prepared for our air attacks and amphibious landings. This has got to cease for us to win this war. . .

"When I heard of this, a light turned on in my head and I said, `Ah hah. No one knows the Navajo language but Navajos.'

"I received permission, after much red tape, and proposed a plan to Marine Corps officers at Camp Elliott just north of San Diego, on February 28, 1942. General Vogel[1] and his staff heard me out and liked my proposal to devise a system composed entirely of Navajo radiomen. They appointed Colonel Wethered Woodward, as the Marine officer in charge, to implement the program.

"Those of you sworn into this program will be called *code talkers*, and I emphasize again, this program is classified *top secret*. You will be the second group trained. The original group of twenty-nine code talkers was sworn in at Ft. Wingate, New Mexico, on October of 1942. They are already in combat areas throughout the Pacific Theater. They came right off of the reservation. Eventually we hope to recruit at least two hundred code talkers and perhaps many more.

"You will complete your Boot Camp training here and then go to Field Signal Battalion Training Center at Oceanside, California. . . Questions. . ."

"How will this code talker program work?" asked a Marine named Betone.

"You will work in teams, using your two-way radio sets. You will convey messages from your officers, maybe asking for reinforcements or calling in coordinates for bombing, etcetera, speaking always in your Navajo tongue."

"But we do not have Navajo words for military words like airplane and tank and those things," commented a Bitsillie boy.

"Good point," said Philip Johnston. "This is where we will improvise and develop new words. All of you can help in implementing this new pigeon Navajo we will use. For example we can refer to airplanes as birds in Navajo, and a Commanding Officer could be a War Chief. Get the idea?"

Sergeant Johnston motioned for a table and chairs to be moved onto the floor. "Okay, now we get to work. Some of you may not qualify for this program and some of you may not wish to be in it. This will be strictly voluntary. I want you to come one at a time. Sit here in front of me. Answer my questions and carry on a five minute conversation with me, speaking only Navajo. Then I want you to write a paragraph that I will dictate to you in English-- English to Navajo, Navajo to English. I want to see how much you already know."

The excitement was high among the Navajo recruits. It poured new incentive and enthusiasm into them to become better Marines. Thus began Clay Walker's initiation into the code talkers. How grateful he was that his friend, Ben Wallowing Bull and his Social Worker, Ted Jacobs had pushed him to learn how to speak, read and write correct American.

THIRTY-EIGHT

Basic Training was completed. Code Talker training was completed. He received his first stripe. He was now Pfc Walker. He was proud of what he had accomplished. Now he wanted to see combat action, which is what they called being in battle. Now Pfc Walker wanted to be a real warrior.

He was going into his first battle. Now he would finally *be* a warrior. Now he would face an enemy whose job was to kill he and his fellow warriors. And he must try to kill them. . . First.

How did he feel? Scared? Tense? Anxious? Perhaps all of these. Perhaps none of these. Perhaps he was numb to any feelings. Just waiting to get on with it. . . Whatever lay out there ahead.

He looked around at his fellow warriors crowded into the landing craft. The best. United States Marines. The Corp. A proud tradition. The most elite warriors in the world. Most were young. It was always the young who fought wars. The young who were wounded, maimed, killed. Older ones started wars. Politicians, governments, vague things like economics, race, greed, suspicion, hatred, lust for power. But it was mostly the young who fought and died.

He couldn't read their thoughts. Probably the same as his. Going into the face of the unknown. Silence. Except for the hum of the motor and the slap of the water against the landing craft. They had been told their objective was named Guadalcanal. Strange name for an island, he thought.

Now the noise came. The boom of big guns reaching out at them from the island. Then the pop, pop of small arms fire. The chatter of automatic weapons. The thump, thump of mortar fire. A close shot sent a geyser of spray over them and rocked their landing craft.

"Stand by to hit the beach!" shouted the platoon leader, a young freckle-faced second lieutenant. "When that ramp goes down, move out!"

The landing craft struck sand. The ramp came down. There it was: The unknown. Guadalcanal. The enemy.

"Go, go, go! Move it!"

The water was to his thighs. He didn't know if it was warm or cold or wet. A harmless looking line of spurts in the water moved toward him. Not harmless. Deadly! Machine gun bullets. They took down two marines beside him. They fell face down in the water. Floated like discarded clothing. The water turned red around them. He stood dumb-like. Transfixed.

"Move it! Hit that beach!" someone shouted behind him, shoving him forward.

Pfc Clay Walker, United States Marine Corp hit the beach in the prone position, his heart thumping in his throat like a drum. Sand kicked up in spurts around him. Marines fell all around him, some screaming in pain for a medic. Some dead. His platoon leader, the freckle-faced lieutenant, spun around in a wild dance and fell dead. Clay knew he was dead from the awkward position of his body. Dead. All dead. Brave warriors all lying dead on the beach. And what good was their bravery, he wondered? What had their death proved? No glory. No hero's welcome home. No family or friends with them. Dead and gone suddenly, and too young to die. This wasn't like counting coup. This was death.

"Dig in! Dig in!" It was a sergeant shouting. He had taken command.

Clay managed to get his entrenching tool off his back and discovered he had lost his walkie talkie in the water coming ashore. Fine mess. Him a "talker" and no talking machine. Didn't matter now. Just stay alive. Frantically he began to dig a hole in the sand. Bullets and mortar rounds still coming in. Too exposed.

"Move out!" shouted the sergeant. "Up farther, into the trees. No good here."

Clay was running, stumbling, crawling. Running again. Trees. Foliage. He fell into some bushes gasping for breath. A tree in front of him. Cover. Hide. Stay alive. He rolled over on his back to rest. Directly above him a weapon pointed at him out of the leaves. He quickly rolled over, firing at the leaves. A body dropped to the ground six feet from him. He fired into the body again. It didn't move. Cautiously he crawled to it. Poked it with his rifle and turned it over. Dead enemy had the face of his friend Takawashi Kami. His friend, Tak, from the Raft. No, this was enemy. His mind whirled in confusion. He began to shake uncontrollably.

"Move out!" the sergeant shouted. "A hundred yards more and dig in for the night."

. . .

Night. Darkness. He didn't remember time passing. He hardly remembered digging the foxhole with the big marine now sharing it with him. From Oklahoma, Clay learned. Big as a horse, he thought.

"I saw you nail that Jap in the tree," said his buddy. "Fast thinking. . . Catch a few winks. I'll take first watch."

The taunts of the enemy. Out there in the dark. The moans of the wounded. He didn't know when sleep came. He couldn't distinguish the nightmares from the real.

. . .

Many nights and many days. Time had no meaning anymore. Besides living with constant fear and the smell of death hanging in the air, there were insects by the millions. Snakes, scorpions, centipedes as long as his arm. Heat, sweat, dirt. How long? How much longer for it to end? Or would it never end?

. . .

Another gray dawn was arriving. "Move out," was whispered down the line of foxholes. Enemy out there. They crawled out of their holes like snakes, wiggling forward on their bellies. Through swarms of insects. Tired, stiff, sore.

Clay heard firing on his right flank. Then silence again. A noise up in front of him. Movement. He froze. Hardly breathing. Twenty yards in front of him the foliage parted. A face crawling toward him. His friend, Tak. No! Enemy! But it was the face of Tak. The face saw him. Tak was bringing his rifle around to point it at Clay.

"No, Tak. It's me, Clay!" he shouted.

But the rifle was almost pointing at him. Pfc Walker's Marine Corp training took over. He brought his own rifle up quickly and fired one round. It made a neat hole in the forehead of the enemy.

He crawled forward and turned the body over. There was no helmet on the head, just an olive green canvas cap with a bill. Unseeing eyes stared up at

feet down. Clay stood transfixed, watching the enemy he had just killed swing slowly back and forth.

He shouted, "Look up! They are in the trees. They have tied themselves in the trees."

Shooting erupted everywhere, mostly small arms fire but an occasional thunk, thunk, of mortar fire. The ground began to erupt around them, spraying dirt. The thunder was deafening. It was the big guns. Clay imagined this is what Hell of the Christians must be like.

"Hit the dirt everyone! Dig in!" Lieutenant Ray Colby was shouting. "Walker over here with me, quick!" Clay and the Lieutenant tumbled into a shell crater. They were breathing heavily. "You okay, Walker?" gasped Colby.

"Yes Sir, Lieutenant. Just scared."

The Marines had taken a lot of territory. Time passed without seeming to. Staying alive took all of their mental and physical energy.

"You didn't look scared," said the Lieutenant, during a lull in the explosions. "You shot that Jap out of the tree as slick as it could have been done."

"Just reflex, I guess, Lieutenant. But I can assure you that I am scared every single minute."

Night was coming and gradually the firing ceased except for a sporadic rifle shot now and then. Clay and Colby hugged the bottom of their shell hole in silence. The bombardment continued, while dirt sprayed upon them until they were almost completely covered.

The Lieutenant whispered, "Walker, I have a terrible hunch that those are our own big guns from our ships off shore. I think that we have overrun our covering fire."

"Could be, Lieutenant. We have moved inland pretty fast."

The cries of the wounded could be heard. Clay spoke in a whisper. "Sometimes the Japs will imitate our wounded. Sometimes they will taunt us in our own language and try to tempt us out of our cover."

"You been on other landings, Walker?"

"Yes, Sir."

"Then you have had your initiation. This is my first. You will have to keep me on the right track."

"You must be doing okay, Lieutenant. You are still alive and the men are still following your orders. I guess it doesn't get any easier. . .the landings and battles, I mean. This one seems even worse than my last, but then memory is short. You begin to wonder how long you can beat the odds and cheat death."

"You are an Indian, a Navajo, I understand. . ."

"Yes, Sir. I am a true reservation Indian. I know very little of your civilization except what I learned in Reform School and Boot Camp. Sometimes I think things are happening to me too fast. I feel like an old man and yet I don't really know what it is all about."

They fell silent. Clay was thinking back to how Ted Jacobs at the Raft had always encouraged him to talk and express his feelings more. He felt a need to express himself now to this friendly officer. Mostly he just needed the comfort of human communication.

"You know, Lieutenant, as far back as I can remember, I wanted to be a warrior. Now that I am a warrior it makes me sick sometimes. My idea of a warrior was a brave young Indian riding a fast horse against a small band of enemy warriors to count coup. Counting coup is when you run or ride up and touch your enemy with a coup stick. This was the bravest act of the warrior. Once in awhile, he might take an enemy scalp or capture some of his horses. Once in a while, he would go for blood, but mostly just for counting coup.

"The type of warriors we are now doesn't meet my old dream of a warrior. Sometimes I feel like I don't even want to kill the enemy. But then I see him killing my fellow warriors. I see the terrible things they have done to innocent civilians. I know it must be me or them."

"Private Walker, you have summed up, I imagine, the feelings of almost every warrior here. I am totally bushed. Will you take the first watch? We can try to get a little shut-eye in shifts."

"Yes, Sir. I don't think I will dare close my eyes all night anyway, after what happened in my last hole at night."

"I heard about that and I don't blame you. I can't think of a worse way to spend a night."

FORTY-ONE

Dawn came with the thunder of big guns and dirt spraying on them. Clay remembered dozing a few times on his sleep shifts. His body ached. He and the Lieutenant broke out a can of C-rations and gulped down their breakfast. They remained pinned down by fire, perhaps from their own guns, for another day and night. Their nerves were raw and their bodies weary.

Lieutenant Colby said, "Walker, I hate to send you, and I won't order you, but will you be a runner back to unit headquarters on the beach?"

"Sure will, Sir. I need to break the monotony of this hole."

"Okay. We need to give them our position and redirect our big gun fire. And we could use another platoon of reinforcements on our right flank. We should be coming up on a town before long if we can get cleared to move out again. Got it?"

"Yes, Sir. I am on my way."

"And be careful. There are probably snipers everywhere."

Clay moved out crawling, stopping suddenly as he bumped into a dead GI. In shock he stared at the shiny samurai sword strapped to his side, the same sword that had killed Begay. A dead warrior with his souvenir. He moved around the body, snaking his way through the undergrowth for twenty minutes until he heard voices talking softly. Parting the fern brush, he saw three Japanese about ten yards away. They looked like they were settled in for awhile, so he detoured around them. He could see the beach about a hundred yards ahead where operation headquarters was established. He was congratulating himself on making it when something hard was jammed into his back and a voice spoke quietly.

"Don't move, Jap, or you are dead. You may not understand me, but I am sure you know a cocked .45 in your back. Hands in the air. . . Up. . . Hands up!"

Pfc Clay Walker raised his hands, scared that the .45 might go off any second. "I am not a Jap," he said. "I am a Marine."

The GI was surprised. "Well, a smart Jap. You speak pretty good English for a Jap."

"You are wrong. I am not a Jap. I am with the 2nd Battalion 5th Marines," Clay managed to explain.

His captor shoved the pistol harder into his back. "I've heard that they plant some of you English speaking Japs as spies to set traps and ambushes. Move! I am taking you into the command post."

"Good. Then maybe someone with sense will listen to me," said Clay nervously.

The captor and his prisoner moved down into the open on the beach and to a hut used as headquarters. The GI approached a Captain seated at an ammunition box desk. "Captain, I captured me a Jap sneaking up on us," he said proudly.

Clay protested again. "Sir, I am not a Jap. I am on your side. . ."

"He tried to give me the same story, Sir. He is a smart one. Speaks good English," cut in the GI.

"Captain, I am a runner, 1st Platoon, A Company, 2nd Battalion, Fifth Marines. Here are my dog tags around my neck. Look for yourself. Clay Walker, Private First Class."

The Captain pulled out his dog tags and examined them while Clay still had his hands in the air. "How come you look like a Jap then?" asked the Captain.

"I didn't realize that I did, Sir. I am a Native American, a Navajo Indian. I am a code talker. . ."

"You are a code talker?" asked the Captain.

"Yes, Sir. Lieutenant Colby of the 1st Platoon sent me as a runner to tell you to extend the gun fire from our ships out there a few clicks high. Some of their fire is hitting us. We are also pinned down by the enemy as well. Some fix, huh? We could also use some reinforcements on our right flank. Call the Lieutenant and he will verify what I have told you, Sir."

"Hand me that phone, Jackson," the Captain barked. He rang for Lieutenant Ray Colby on the radio transmitter. "Lieutenant Colby, this is Captain Schultz at command post. Did you send a Pfc Walker here as a runner?"

"Yes, Sir. Did he make it? Is he hurt?"

"Yes, he made it and no he is not hurt. He was captured by one of my men who thought he was a Jap. I understand he is a code talker?"

"That is right, Sir."

"Then why in hell don't you use him as one, Lieutenant? Code talkers are not to be used as runners. He could have relayed your message in fifteen seconds, that probably took hours on foot. We have a two man code talker team here at headquarters. We have them all over the island and also on our battleships and aircraft carriers. . . Read your instruction manual. Don't ever use code talkers as runners again. Got it, Lieutenant?"

"Yes, Sir."

"I am sending Walker back to you with a bodyguard. And in the future I will send out an order that all code talkers have body guards, especially since they are mistaken as Japs. . . And we will correct the big gun fire. Thanks, Lieutenant. I will also see what I can do about help on your right flank."

The Captain turned to the sheepish looking GI who had captured Pfc Clay Walker. "Corporal, since this man is your prisoner I am sending you to guard him all the way back to his unit. If he gets so much as a scratch on him, don't bother coming back. Only kidding, Corporal. You did right by bringing him in. It is best not to take chances. Get going now."

The Corporal and Clay made it safely back to Colby's platoon. Clay slid into the foxhole with Lieutenant Colby and said sheepishly, "Sorry about the trouble I caused, Lieutenant. I avoided lots of the enemy, but got captured by our own troops."

"That is rather embarrassing. It won't happen again. It was my fault. I didn't know exactly how to use you."

"It was partly my fault, Lieutenant. I should have explained what I can do. We Navajos are backward sometimes and I didn't want to overstep my authority. I know, despite what the Captain said, that you don't have time for reading your manual out here."

Lieutenant Colby was thoughtful for awhile and then asked, "Is it true that you can relay messages faster than any other method? How long does it take you to decode a message received?"

"It is decoded when I write it down. The translating is done in my head. You didn't know much about us because our operation is so new and classified. Many officers are just learning. You are not alone. The Japanese had previously broken every one of our codes, so someone finally discovered us Navajos. Our language is a difficult one. The Japanese know nothing about it. So there are teams of us all over the islands. We talk to each other, conveying the messages of our officers in our native language."

"Thanks for the lesson, Private Walker. I am glad to have you with me to keep me honest."

"No problem, Sir."

Dusk was coming again. They would spend another night dug in. Just before darkness descended, Lieutenant Colby broke the silence.

"Walker, stick your helmet on your rifle and hoist it up. Let's see if we got those reinforcements on our right flank."

Clay did as instructed and rifle fire zinged over their heads.

"Yep, reinforcements are there," said Colby smiling. "It is a green army platoon. The Captain said it would be their first time in battle. They shoot at anything and everything. So watch out."

"That puts us in a hot place, Lieutenant," said Clay. "Friends shooting at us from our right flank, enemy from our left flank and in front of us. It should be an interesting night."

F O R T Y - T W O

Pfc Clay Walker had dozed off when static on his radio receiver woke him. A voice gave the code name *Arizona* and identified himself as a code talker from command headquarters. He read a short message and signed off. Clay wrote it down and handed the paper to Lieutenant Ray Colby: *Move out toward objective at 0600.*

"Okay, Walker, pass the word down the line for everyone to be ready to move out at 0600 hours."

They opened some C-rations and gulped down beans and vienna sausage for breakfast, washing it down with four swigs of warm water, all the time swatting at mosquitoes that swarmed around them like small dive bombers.

Ray Colby peered over the edge of the foxhole and chuckled aloud. "Did you hear our army buddies firing at that noise in the brush out in front of us last night?"

"Yeah, I heard that."

"Well take a look. They got one of the enemy. . .an enemy pig."

About twenty yards out in front of them lay a dead wild pig. They both laughed again. "Better a dead pig than taking chances," said the Lieutenant.

The dawn was unusually quiet. The hum of insects grew louder. Lieutenant Colby looked at his watch and said softly to his men in the next foxhole, "Okay, move out. Pass the word."

Heads came out of foxholes on down the line. Troops began to advance quietly through the jungle. Most of the morning they moved steadily forward without encountering the enemy. Suddenly they broke free of the jungle into a clearing. There was a village, with houses lining narrow streets. Aslito Airfield should be just beyond.

Shots came from a window in the first house and two GIs were hit. The rest took cover and returned fire. Through hand signals, Lieutenant Colby sent one squad on each side of the narrow street leading between two rows of houses. He led the third squad as they cautiously started moving down the street from house to house.

A Jap jumped out of a doorway using an old civilian lady as a shield. Just as he opened fire, Clay yelled, "Look out, Lieutenant," and pushed him to the ground, at the same time falling with him.

The Marine next to them returned fire killing the Jap and also the old woman. He muttered to himself, "Oh no. Oh no. . . But. . . There was no other way."

Other Japanese came out of the huts, using civilians as shields, as shooting erupted everywhere. Clay and Colby got to their feet and ran for cover behind a fence.

"Thanks, Walker, you saved my life. . . Those cowardly rats are using innocent civilians as human shields. How horrible. We will kill them too or get killed ourselves." Then he looked at Clay. "You have been hit, Walker."

"It is just a scratch," said Clay, wincing in pain.

"Let me take a look," said Colby. "Scratch, my fanny. You've got a shattered wrist, and you are bleeding like a stuck pig. . . Medic! Medic!" he shouted over his shoulder.

A medic came on the run and knelt beside Clay. "Here, buddy, let me stop that bleeding first; then I'll give you a shot of morphine for the pain. . . He ought to be evacuated, Lieutenant," he said to Colby.

"Can you help him back to the command post, medic?"

"Yes, Sir. I can be spared. We have several other medics available."

Turning to Clay, Colby said, "Walker, I hate like crazy to lose you, but you are no good with a shattered wrist, and you could bleed to death, so I've got to send you to the rear. . . If you heal up quick enough, I will work some way out to get you back as my code talker." Then he clapped Clay on his good shoulder and added, "Thanks again for your quick thinking or I might not be here myself."

"That's okay, Lieutenant. It gave me a chance to rough up an officer," Clay said smiling.

Pfc Walker and the medic made it back to command post. The doctor there looked at his wound and frowned. "It is a bad looking wrist, Private. I am going to evacuate you to the hospital ship out in the bay."

Walks Two Worlds, had received his first wound in battle, and he hoped his last. He had seen much death and pain in others. Now he felt the pain in his own body.

FORTY-THREE

He returned to consciousness slowly, not knowing what world he was in. He saw steel bulkheads, steel overhead and steel deck, all gray. He felt a gentle rolling motion, and his memory began to return. The memories were not happy ones. War left wounds and scars much deeper than the physical ones. He was still just a teenager and he had already seen too much pain and death to assimilate it. Even now, after many battles, he did not understand fully what this war was about. *Walks Two Worlds*, the warrior, was becoming disillusioned with his lifetime dream. War and the warrior were not the same as his dreams of them had been.

A doctor came in and took his pulse. He looked at the chart on the clipboard hanging from the foot of the bed, then asked, "How is the wrist feeling, Private Walker?"

"It throbs clear up to the shoulder."

"That is probably a good sign. You still have feeling in it. I was able to tie the veins and arteries together, repair the broken bones and get out most of the chips. The bad news is that you may have some nerve damage. I am having you evacuated back to Honolulu, Hawaii, where they have better facilities than we have here on the ship. You will more than likely have to have further surgery. But the prognosis is good; your hand will at least be saved. So hang in there, Son. And good luck to you."

Clay Walker remembered little about his first airplane flight ever. He was too sedated. He kept fading in and out of reality. Often the dream world was more real.

FORTY-FOUR

Pfc Clay Walker returned to the conscious world, again not knowing where he was. It took him a few minutes to reorganize thoughts in his mind. His arm was in an awkward cast. There was no motion, so he was not on the ship. Everything was clean and white. White sheets and pillow case on his white bed. Then he remembered someone saying that he was being sent to Honolulu for more surgery.

A picture on the wall caught his attention. Ironically it was a framed photo in black and white of Monument Valley, his own Navajoland. The photograph was taken by the famous photographer Ansel Adams. Clay's mind traveled back in time to furnish the colors to the photo. His grandfather was once again speaking to the small boy, Clay Walker: "Time stands still in this land, my son. Its beauty never fades. How I love its colors, its sky. It is my land. . ."

Thinking of his home, tears welled up in his eyes and ran down the sides of his face. How he missed his grandfather who had gone on to the Great Mystery. His grandfather's words, summarizing their land, returned vividly to his mind: "Many people think a desert is just a desert, as if that was explanation for drabness. Not so, my boy. A desert is alive with beauty. . ."

. . .

A doctor entered the room to break off his reverie.

"How is the arm, Son? Hurt much?" the doctor asked.

"It is okay as far as I know. I can't feel much."

"Well I can give you the good news that the surgery was successful," said the doctor while taking Clay's blood pressure. "We were able to reconstruct your wrist and hand, and repair most of the nerve damage. I feel confident that you will have ninety percent use of your hand again. You should be like new in two, maybe three or four weeks at the most. I will drop in when I can.

But I know that nurse will take good care of you. Of all her patients she especially likes you, I think."

As the doctor was leaving, a tall Marine officer with graying sideburns entered. He and the doctor nodded at each other.

"I am Major Rolfe, Son," said the officer. "How are you making it? You look a little pale and your eyes are red. . ."

"I am okay, Major. I have just been crying over all of the dead Marines. And maybe crying a little for myself. I have been missing my homeland. It is there in that picture on the wall."

The Major looked at the picture. Clay's honesty brought an awkward silence, as the Major bowed his head for a few moments. "These are little compensation, Private Walker, but they might help brighten you up a bit and ease your pain." He placed two medals on the pillow by Clay's head. "A Purple Heart and a Bronze Star. Lieutenant Colby stated in his commendation how you had saved his life."

Clay picked up the medals one at a time with his good hand and held them up so he could see them. "Thank you, Sir. Lieutenant Colby is a good officer."

"He said he wants you back with him when you are healed." The Major turned to leave, stopped and faced Clay again. "I almost forgot. You will need to stop at the PX and get yourself another stripe to sew on your arm, *Corporal* Walker. You have been promoted."

Corporal Walker managed a smile and thanked the Major again. He imagined that getting another stripe must be like an ancestor warrior getting another feather in his hair. He chuckled to himself.

FORTY-FIVE

Nurse Gayle Stoker came into his room smiling. She had made it a point to drop in everyday to see how he was doing, and stay to talk a while.

"How is my favorite Navajo doing?" she asked.

"Favorite, because I am the only Navajo you have ever known?"

They both laughed, because the first time he had to tell her he was a Navajo, an American Indian. She had guessed Hawaiian, Mexican, Samoan and the vague designation Oriental. So he had told her about being captured by American troops on Saipan, who thought he was the Japanese enemy. Clay liked Nurse Stoker. She was not pretentious. Besides, she was pretty, petite, and made him feel good. She had eyes the color of a clear sky and her hair was like sunshine.

"How is the wrist? Can you move the fingers?. . . Show me."

"Sure can. See. Feels okay too."

"Great. Doctor says the cast can come off next week." She sat on the edge of his bed. "Have you ever seen Pearl Harbor, been out there I mean? It is where this war all started."

"No. The first time I ever heard of it was the day I raised my hand to join the Marine Corps."

"Would you like to go out there with me? Doctor says you ought to get out of here for some fresh air and exercise. And you really need to see the place that started all the fighting you have been in. Someday it will be a patriotic slogan like `Remember the Alamo.' It will be `Remember Pearl Harbor.' You will see."

"Yes, I would like to go with you. I would like that very much."

"Okay, be spruced up and looking your best tomorrow morning at ten. I have a car. I will drive us out."

. . .

Gayle Stoker came into his room at ten sharp. He was still struggling to get into his shirt with his awkward cast.

"Here, let me give you a hand with that. You are making it far too difficult," she said, slipping his shirt on over the sling and cast.

He looked embarrassed.

"Don't be shy. You should have seen what I helped you with when you were unconscious. I have helped many GIs get dressed with more awkward casts than yours."

"You must have seen some bad ones, huh?"

"That I have. I had just finished nursing school back in California when the war started and I thought that I could be of most help here in Oahu. It was a shock at first. It is very rewarding to be helping a little. . . Here, slip your one arm into your jacket now and I will button it and you are all set."

She stepped back and surveyed him. "Wow, what a handsome dude you are in your uniform. Come on, we have a big day."

Clay began to relax in the car. The city of Honolulu was bustling with activity. Soon they left the traffic of the city and were driving along palm tree and bougenvilla lined highways.

"I have never been alone with a pretty *belagaana* woman before," he said quietly.

"You make me sound mysterious. What is it that you called me?"

"*Belagaana*. It just means White or anything that isn't *Dineh*. We Navajos are *Dineh*, which means *The People*. . .like we have been around forever, which maybe we have."

"You look awfully young, Clay, to be in the Marines, and yet you have been through terrible battles and seen horrible things. . . How old are you?"

"Everybody tells me that I look too young. Maybe because I am little. I spent a long time in Reform School when I first came to the White World. They called me Little Injun there. That was where I joined the Marines. We called it the Raft. It was the only real home I have had in the White World."

There was a silence while she gave him time to collect his thoughts.

"How old am I? Maybe eighteen or nineteen. I don't know. I was born in a hogan with a dirt floor. Records weren't kept much on the reservation. Time was not an important thing to us Navajos. All I know is what my grandfather and my uncles have told me. I was raised mostly by them. I feel that I am older than my grandfather. I feel that I have lived for many years beyond my age. That is weird, huh?"

Nurse Stoker glanced at him often, as though studying him while they drove along. "Tell me about your grandfather and life on the reservation," she said hesitantly, not wanting to pry too soon.

Clay waited a spell before replying. "He was called White Horse after a famous ancestor who was also known as White Horse. He died just before I left the reservation. I still feel his *chindi* close to me, talking to me, talking inside of my head. . . That is his ghost or spirit. He was my *hataalii*, my teacher, the wise one who instructs me in the ways I should walk. I was his student in learning the old ways. He was lean, tall, and his hair was long and silver, like moonlight. He was parent, brother and friend to me."

She smiled, a warm understanding smile. "I like to hear you talk. You talk like a poet or philosopher."

"I don't know about those things. I have very little school learning. It was only a short time ago that I learned to talk your language. I have Reform School and the Marine Corps to thank for what little I know of your ways. I am still learning much."

"We all are learning, or at least should be learning always," she added.

"Life on the reservation was hard and yet easy. It is not to be explained in words," he continued. "I loved the *Dinetah*, our land of sand, sagebrush, yucca and red mountains. Our lives were a struggle for food and survival. We planted a few things that would grow in that country: corn, beans, squash. And we herded sheep and goats. I liked the long days of sunshine. There was time to think and time to enjoy what the Gods had given to us. We had little contact with your world of modern devises. I am ashamed to say that I cannot drive a car. I am glad that you offered to drive."

They both laughed.

Gayle Stoker announced, "Here we are. Pearl Harbor."

A guard checked their credentials at the gate and waved them onto the docks where Nurse Stoker parked the car. She helped him out and led the way to the wharf.

"This is what was once mighty battleship row," she said, sweeping her hand out along the harbor. "This is what the Japanese bombed in their surprise attack on December 7, 1941. They literally wiped out our fleet right here. If our aircraft carriers had not been at sea, we couldn't have recovered to retaliate at the battle of Midway. There we got even and turned the tide of the war."

"You know a lot about the war," he commented.

"I have studied. And I have learned from our boys who come to the hospital and from the locals who were here when it happened. It is my duty to know. You see they are rebuilding, but it will take time. See that activity out there," she said, pointing. "They are marking the spot where the Arizona sunk with one thousand, one hundred and seventy-seven of our men still buried inside the watery tomb."

Clay pondered upon this, trying to comprehend so many men killed on one ship. The thought overwhelmed him.

"Over there," Nurse Stoker continued explaining, "on the other side of Ford Island, is where the battleship Utah went down with over fifty men still on board. . .I am sure that some day they will build a memorial marking the tomb of the Arizona."

"Ironic," he remarked. "My home. . ."

"What do you mean?" she asked, puzzled.

"Arizona and Utah. . . The battleships named after my home. That is where the reservation lies. . . It is my home."

They fell silent in thought as they walked along, surveying the destruction and construction side by side. Clay spoke, as though still trying to solve a problem that perplexed him. "You know, I look upon all of this destruction and think of all of the deaths caused by this evil Japanese empire. . . And yet in Reform School, in the Raft as we called it, one of my best friends was a Jap kid named Takawashi Kami. We called him Tak. A nicer guy and more loyal friend couldn't be found. I haven't quite sorted it all out in my mind yet."

"We often put a judgment upon a whole race or nation, Clay, forgetting that each nation is made up of individuals; and all of them are not evil or good. They are just people." They came to a small concession stand for dock workers. "Let's get an ice cream cone," she suggested. "Do you like ice cream?"

"I love it," said Clay. "It is one food of the White World that I can never get enough of."

He got vanilla. Gayle got chocolate. Corporal Walker pulled out a handful of money and handed it to the vendor. He said to Nurse Stoker, "This money is something I know little about and have little use for. I never saw it on the reservation and you don't need it in the Pacific island jungles where I have been."

"Most people in our so-called civilization have it as the main goal in their lives," Gayle said. "To get as much of it as they can. . . They often would stab each other in the back to get it," she said scornfully. They walked in silence, licking their ice creams. Finally Gayle Stoker said, "Shall we head back to the car?"

"I hate for this time to end," said Clay Walker. "This day has been more enjoyable than I can remember in a long time. There should be many more days like this. . . And it is you, Nurse Gayle Stoker, that has made it extra special for me."

"I feel the same way, Clay. It is too bad that we can't say for sure that there will be more days like it."

She reached over and kissed him on the cheek.

FORTY-SIX

Temporary duty at Scofield became tedious; the inactivity was boring. Corporal Clay Walker's wound had healed. His wrist, his hand worked well again. Only two fingers were still difficult to regain their movement. His assignment was in quartermaster where he inventoried and helped hand out uniforms and equipment to new GIs coming to the base. Evenings were spent in games at the rec hall or movies. He had too much time to think. He must write a long overdue letter to his uncles, Sits By The Fire and Happy Jack. He would address it to them in care of the Indian Agent or the Tribal Council.

He didn't like to write letters, although he had written a couple to his Social Worker Ted Jacobs, who had helped him so much, and a couple to Big Injun. He had lost track of Ben Wallowing Bull since he had gone somewhere overseas. What do you say to people whose worlds have become so different from your own? You swear to never change, to remain yourself. But who is your real self? You discover that you are not one self, but many constantly evolving selves. Perhaps nothing ever remains the same except the mountains and the land. Maybe that is as it should be.

But this letter was an obligation, a duty letter that he must write.

To my Uncles—

I am sorry that I have not written to you before. I was ashamed to write for a long time since I felt that I was a disappointment to you and the council.

At first I shamed the name *Walks Two Worlds*, not because I meant to, but because I didn't understand this *belagaana* world to which you sent me against my wishes. I have learned much of this world. I now read, write and speak well in the language of the White Man.

I think that I have now made right many of the mistakes that I made at first. The *Dineh* can perhaps be proud of me as I am now a warrior in the U.S. Marine Corps. They are the best warriors the White Man has. I was wounded while fighting the enemy of America. My wound taught me of pain. I am now recovering after being in the hospital in the Hawaiian Islands. Perhaps I will be sent into battle again. If I survive this war maybe I will see my homeland again and talk with you, my uncles.

What more can I do to learn of the White World than to fight with his warriors and perhaps to die with him in battle. I hope that this news maybe will make you proud of me. I miss the Dineh and my homeland and hope that I may see it again.

Your nephew and friend to all,
Clay Walker (*Walks Two Worlds*)

He folded the letter and sealed it without reading it. It was done. Now, if he made it through the war he could walk proudly among his people at home in *Dinetah*.

The following day a messenger summoned him to base headquarters.

"Corporal Walker, reporting as ordered, Sir." He snapped a salute to the colonel sitting behind the desk.

"At ease, Corporal. It looks like your TDY is over. This may be good news or bad news, depending on your outlook. You are to report back to your old unit, 2nd Battalion, 5th Marine Division. A Lieutenant Ray Colby wants you as his aid and code talker. They are still on Saipan, which is now secured and in our hands. So you will at least have a breather from combat."

He handed the orders to Clay, adding, "You have been in some tough battles I see by your records, Son. So I wish you the very best, and good luck to you."

FORTY-SEVEN

Corporal Clay Walker's second landing on Saipan was much different than the first. It was smooth and peaceful, as the four engine bomber rolled to a stop on the repaired Aslito runway. There were seabees still driving heavy equipment, moving earth for more hangars and buildings. Clay was astounded at the change.

He shouldered his duffle bag and was directed towards the headquarters building. He entered to find Lieutenant Ray Colby sitting behind a make-shift desk.

"Corporal Clay Walker reporting for duty, Sir," he said, saluting.

The Lieutenant looked up and returned his salute with a smile. Then he came around his desk and warmly shook Clay's hand. "Good to have you back, Corporal. I told you I would get you back here. How is the hand? Let me see it."

Clay stuck it out, moving it around. "Almost like new, Sir. Just a couple of stiff fingers. They will loosen up when I get back to work. . . How did you do it?" asked Clay.

"Do what?"

"Get me assigned back to you. How did you pull it off?"

"I just told them that I would not settle for a greeny, that you were the best at your job," Colby replied. Then he added, "And it didn't hurt to have a favorite uncle in a high diplomatic job in Washington."

"And your gold bars have turned to silver on your collar," said Clay. "You are now a first Lieutenant."

"They are hard up for officers. I guess they are scraping the bottom of the barrel. Come on, I'll show you around. Leave your duffel bag here. I'll get you to your barracks later."

"Barracks. . . You mean that we actually have beds now, Sir?"

"Not exactly beds, but a lot better than holes in the ground. . . Speaking of holes in the ground, do you want to try a shift in one tonight to get back in shape? We still have a few fanatic snipers hiding out in the jungles. They got one of our guys a week ago. You don't have to, you know. I can get you light duty for a few days to adjust. . ."

"I'll take my turn, Sir. I want to be a part of the unit again."

"Still the A-1 best warrior, huh?"

"I have to be, Lieutenant. It is all I know how to do except herd sheep and goats," Clay said, smiling.

"You have seen the airfield," continued Colby. "Our construction engineers are doing a great job. They are widening and extending the main runway. Our pilots will soon be dropping bombs on Japan. They are also putting up more barracks, maintenance sheds, offices, everything. We will have a regular city here.

"After you left us, we had another three weeks or so of fighting. Things didn't get better for a long while. The Japs kept using civilians as shields. It was bad. Many innocent people got killed, people who really had nothing to do with this war and didn't even know what it was all about. And then some real fanatical Japs started using themselves as human bombs. They would pull the pin on a grenade or strap dynamite to their backs and run into our lines. . .

"You saw our fancy steel flag pole back there at command post. It was probably shipped clear from Akron, Ohio. Well our first flag, when we took the island, went up way out there," he said, pointing. "Follow that line of telephone poles. . . The last one was our flag pole. That is called Marpi Point. We raised the flag there on July 9, 1944. Like I say, we own this island now. But be awake tonight on watch. There are still some maniacs out there. We have lost three or four of our seabees to snipers while they have been working on their machines."

FORTY-EIGHT

Clay shared the foxhole that night with a Private Kunz. Their hole was on the far perimeter at the end of the airfield. "We can both stay awake," said Kunz. We don't sleep in shifts anymore. We get relieved in four hours."

"That is another improvement since I have been gone," said Clay.

The time ticked by slowly. An occasional night bird sounded a mournful call. The breeze in the tree leaves made them tense up once in awhile. The mosquitoes were as bad as ever. Clay reflected back to the terrifying night his partner had been killed by a samurai wielding Jap. He wasn't about to relax for a second. Suddenly out of the stillness came a THUNK into their foxhole.

Kunz yelled, "Grenade!"

Clay searched frantically with his hands but couldn't find it. He expected any second to be blown to bits. He found his red lensed flashlight and switched it on towards his partner, who was curled up in the bottom of their foxhole awaiting death. There, staring straight at him, were two sleepy eyes attached to a fat green body the size of a baseball mitt. Perched peacefully on Kunz's back was the biggest bull frog he had ever seen. He started laughing with relief.

"What are you laughing at? Just because it was a dud grenade. . . It might just as easily have killed us," said a panicky Kunz.

The frog hopped off of Kunz's back and croaked a few times, blinking its eyes as if to say, "What is all the fuss about?"

"Look," said Clay, shining his light on it.

"Holy Moses," said Kunz. "It is the biggest whopper of a frog that I have ever seen."

The tension was broken as they both laughed until tears streamed down their cheeks.

. . .

The weeks and months of island occupation duty turned to boredom for the troops. Then one morning, Lieutenant Colby mustered his platoon in front of their headquarters. Other platoons were doing the same.

"We have received new orders," he began. "And I am afraid that they are not what we had hoped for. They are not for R & R, I can tell you that much. You might prefer the boredom I have heard gripes about, instead of what we have coming. I can tell you that we will soon be headed into another tough battle, a big one. That is all the info I am authorized to give out at this time.

"I want to take this opportunity to tell you how proud I am of our platoon on this campaign. Over all, I have heard very little griping. You that were in the battles for possession of this island performed admirably. You new men have had the best training there is, and I know that you will measure up to our standards. We are a close unit. We stick together and get the job done. We miss our buddies who have gone beyond. . .." His voice broke slightly.

"The good news is that we have one week to get our gear packed, our equipment in top shape, and to lay around and get fat and lazy. Dismissed."

Clay looked around as the platoon broke ranks. The Lieutenant was right; there were many new faces. Many of the old faces were gone, gone to join the Great Mystery. He asked himself who would be next? Were his own odds running out? Would he be among the missing faces soon?

FORTY-NINE

The landing craft were circling the larger ship, waiting until all craft were loaded with men and ready to align and assault the beach in waves. Corporal Clay Walker crouched in his craft beside Lieutenant Ray Colby. They were in the second wave. *Walks Two Worlds* was now a seasoned warrior and was approaching yet another battle. What a tremendous war party he was with, more men and machines than he had ever seen together at one time.

"This must be a big one, Lieutenant. What is the name of the place again?" asked Clay, more nervous than ever because he now had an idea of what to expect.

"Iwo Jima," answered Colby. "You are right. This is going to be a big operation. Ground, air, and sea combined, the full works."

"They all begin to look the same. . . These islands, I mean," said Clay.

"This one is more mountainous. Take a look while we are still out of range."

Clay looked over the rim of the craft toward the island. Gray clouds hung ominously over it. It was February, 1945.

"See that tallest mountain," said the Lieutenant, pointing. "The one with the clouds covering its peak. . . That is Mount Suribachi. That is our main objective. We have to reach the top and take it at all cost. Once the top of Suribachi is ours, the rest of the island will just be a mop-up operation."

"You say that we are to take it at any cost?" asked Clay.

"Those are our orders."

"Do you ever think that the cost of something might be too high, too much, Lieutenant?"

Colby gave Clay a strange look and was quiet so long that Clay thought he was ignoring his question. Then he looked into Clay's eyes and replied. "I think about it a lot, Corporal. I think that too often the politicians, and even our high military leaders, begin to speak of cost as if it were just money and supplies and arms, instead of individual fighting men with names, faces and personalities. . . But then on the other hand we are Marines, warriors as you call us. We have a job to do, the most dangerous job there is, a war which we didn't start that has to be won. . . Idealistic view maybe, but I think that we have the greatest country in the world, and I am willing to place my life on the line for it." He looked at Clay harder. "Not thinking of copping out on me are you?"

"No way, Lieutenant. I am with you all the way. Like you said, I am a warrior. . . I just start thinking that the odds increase with each battle. . . That maybe our number might come up."

Colby's brow furrowed in thought. "I know. Probably every warrior has the same thoughts. But we can't dwell upon it or it will hinder our effectiveness. We've got to think of just the task at hand, the immediate job. . . Okay, everyone down. We are starting our approach to the beach. Lock and load your weapons."

Just the purr of the craft's motor and the swish of water could be heard for several minutes that seemed like an eternity. Then thunder, lightning and fire broke loose from the shore. Water spurted up and splashed down on them. The craft next to them took a direct hit and was blown out of the water. Bullets began to ping off their craft.

"Get ready to drop the gate," shouted Lieutenant Colby. "Hit it on the run."

They came off the craft into two feet of water. Some men were hit and died before they reached the sand. Bodies were floating in the water, and the beach was already littered with dead and wounded. Clay made it to the high tide mark on the beach where he hit the sand and was able to crawl to the bush and tree cover. His head was pounding wildly. Like a robot trained to react, he began immediately to string out his wire and rig his radio communications system. Fifty yards ahead, the Lieutenant was on his belly waving for Clay to join him. Crawling through heavy fire, Clay reached him.

"You got that talkie ready to work, Corporal?"

"Yes, Sir. She is ready to talk and receive."

"Call in some mortar fire of our own. We have a mortar squad and a machine gun squad on our left flank. Tell them to blaze away at will a hundred yards to our front. It may give us some breathing space."

The Marines fought for every inch, every foot, every yard. Every day the cost was getting higher in human lives that could not be replaced with money. What they had been told would take probably a few days, was running into weeks. Army and Marine units had fought their way through jungles, land mines and murderous fire, to finally arrive at the base of Mt. Suribachi. Then, at still a higher cost, they were on their way up. The enemy was dug into holes, caves, rocks, like ants in a giant ant hill.

FIFTY

Nerves and stamina had been tested to the ultimate. But still the test continued. It was the second or third week of fighting. Steadily, Corporal Clay Walker's platoon, its numbers badly depleted, was still moving up the volcanic mountain. They were over half way to the top when they again came under heavy fire. Bullets buzzed through the air like angry bees, kicking up the ash and dust around them. Mortars thumped, spraying them with ash and shrapnel. Their platoon was reduced by a third through casualties.

Platoon leader Colby shouted, "Hit the dirt! Dig in!"

Clay tumbled into a shell crater. Another GI fell in on top of him and exclaimed, "Wow, that was close." He turned to look into the face of his new partner and was momentarily stunned. "No! It can't be. I don't believe it. Little Injun? Is it really you?"

Clay explored the face beside him, equally astonished. "Rusty Red! Can this be?"

They hugged each other, tears streaming down their faces while bullets whined overhead.

Rusty Red gained his composure. "Miracle of miracles. What a place to meet. You are finally a warrior, Little Injun. What do you think about it?"

"I think that my dream of being a warrior was maybe a nightmare, huh?"

They both laughed at having met in such an unlikely place and time.

"You can say that again. What outfit are you with?" asked Rusty Red.

"Fifth Marines, Second Battalion. . . I see you got three stripes. A Sergeant, huh?"

"You know me. I can talk my way into most things. I'm with the First Marines on this trip."

They talked and shared C-rations as dusk came. The sky darkened, their talk subdued; but they had so much they wanted to share with each other.

"Do you ever think of Tak?" Clay asked.

"Yeah. Often I think and wonder about him. I hear they are doing bad things to the Japanese back in the States, putting them all in prisons or camps. . .Just because they are Japs."

"It is hard for me to sort it all out in my mind, Rusty Red. Tak, he was a good friend. We were on the run together. Best guy ever. And yet these Japs we are fighting. . . Most of them seem to be real bad ones. On Saipan they used civilians, old people, as human shields. . . And other horrible things they would do. . ."

"That keeps me wondering too, Little Injun." Rusty Red thought awhile and then added, "I guess it is best to not get ourselves too full of hate from what we have seen in this war. And maybe still try to judge each individual for what he is and not lump everyone together. These are deep things that will take more than me or you to sort out."

"I guess you are right, Rusty Red. We have sure had to grow up fast since Raft days, huh?"

"We sure have. . . It's pretty dark; we better get some shut eye. You want first watch duty or me?"

"I only sleep with one eye anyway since I had a foxhole buddy killed one night. . . You sleep first, Sergeant Rusty Red. You outrank me."

They chuckled softly. "Rank means nothing between us," said Rusty Red. "We know too much about each other."

Gradually the night sounds took over. Mostly these sounds were the groans and cries of the wounded and dying.

FIFTY-ONE

With the first rays of dawn, Clay heard a voice calling, "Arizona, Arizona."

He shook Rusty Red's shoulder. "Lieutenant Colby is calling my code signal. Crawl after me and I will introduce you to my platoon leader. He is an okay guy."

Clay slid out of the hole with Rusty Red following. They tumbled into a large foxhole about twenty yards away.

"I see you made it through another night, Walker. We just about have it made now. We'll take this hill today, maybe."

"Lieutenant, this is. . . I don't even know your real name, Rusty Red. All this time and I don't even know your name."

"Sergeant Tolman," said the redhead, shaking hands with the Lieutenant.

"Sergeant Tolman, huh," said Clay. "Well you are still Rusty Red to me. Lieutenant, the Sergeant here. . .me and him grew up together in Reform School."

They all laughed.

"Okay guys. Today we take the top of Suribachi, do or die. Walker, I want you to contact one of your code talkers on the big battle wagon out there in the bay and have them open up a salvo like we have never seen before, at say 0700. Then tell that code talker to relay to that flat top out in the bay to follow up with an air strike at 0800. Here are the coordinates I have been given by the CO." He handed Clay a paper with the necessary information. "Okay Arizona, do your code talker thing."

Clay slipped naturally into his Navajo tongue, while Rusty Red looked on proudly. Suddenly Clay's eyes opened wide and he began to chatter excitedly. Rusty Red heard his name among the chatter.

"It is Big Injun," said Clay incredulously. "Yeah, can you believe it? It is Big Injun right out there on the battle ship. I told him you are right here in the foxhole with me."

Rusty Red explained to Lieutenant Colby, "It is another of our buddies from Reform School, Lieutenant. Can you imagine the odds of this happening? The other code talker out there on the battle wagon was Corporal Walker's best friend at Reform School. We called him Big Injun and this guy Little Injun."

Colby laughed delightedly, as Clay chattered. It took the fate and coincidence of war to bring them together under these unbelievable conditions. Finally Colby said, "Okay, you guys, we have to cut the school reunion short, as much as I hate to. We still have a war to fight. But give your buddy Big Injun the info and also my best regards."

A few minutes after Clay's message, all hell broke loose. Big shells from the sixteen inch guns began to scream over their heads and explode with deafening thunder on the mountain above them. Then as it stopped, the buzz of airplanes came overhead, dropping their bombs. Two of the planes didn't pull out of their dives in time and crashed in huge fireballs just below the peak.

"That's the way I would like to go," muttered Lieutenant Colby quietly. "Quick. Never knowing what hit me."

"Do you think it is like that for them. . . I mean not knowing. . .just suddenly gone?" asked Rusty Red.

"I think it would be like that," said Clay. "I think it would be like going through a door from this world to the next one. My grandfather believed it was that way."

"Well I hope none of us have to know too soon. I still like this world too much, although it is hell right now," said Rusty Red. "It is the only world I know. Lieutenant, we have been here on this mountain around five weeks. They told us it would be ours in three days. You got any opinions when we will take it?" asked Rusty Red.

"Tomorrow. We take the mountain top tomorrow," said Colby. Then he added, "Maybe even today. Yes, maybe today."

Just then a bullet clipped off the antenna on Clay's radio. They all ducked lower in the hole.

"It is good we won't need that anymore, Corporal. You can leave it here and we can move faster for the final assault. Check your weapons and ammo and let's get ready. After that pounding, I don't know how anything could be left alive on that mountain."

FIFTY-TWO

They were wrong. The enemy came out of their holes everywhere, like ants. They were under rocks, in caves, concealed. They would have to be blown and burned out.

Platoon leader Colby shouted, "Move out! Let's take the high ground. Everyone move out and up that mountain."

They were met by small arms fire, the bullets kicking black sand and ash. They ignored the withering fire and kept moving, all units of Marines and Army, the final assault on Mt. Suribachi. Corporal Clay Walker was to the right of Lieutenant Ray Colby, and Sergeant Rusty Red Tolman slightly behind them. They fired as they advanced. They could see the top of the mountain fifty yards or less above them.

An enemy machine gun opened up on their left flank. Its burst hit the Lieutenant and Clay, twisting their bodies and slamming them to the ground. Rusty Red knelt, pulled the pin on a hand grenade and threw it in a high arch over some rocks. Its explosion silenced the machine gun. He ran and knelt by the Lieutenant, then ran over to Clay, who was lying on his back at an awkward angle.

He put his head close to his friend. "Are you hit bad, Little Injun?"

"I think that I am. I can't move much of anything. How is Lieutenant Colby?"

"He is dead."

Clay choked back a sob. "He was a mighty fine officer and a brave warrior. He was my friend."

"Medic! Medic, over here!" screamed Rusty Red over his shoulder. Then he turned back to Clay. "You are a brave warrior, my Little Injun friend. Do you hear me?" he asked, as his eyes blurred and tears overflowed, running down his cheeks.

"I hear you. . . Do you really mean that, Rusty Red?" gasped Clay, his breathing becoming difficult.

"I mean it like I have never meant anything before."

A medic slid in beside them and quickly assessed Clay's wounds. "All I can do for you now partner, is give you a big shot of morphine. We'll get a stretcher here soon as we can and get you off this mountain. . . You look tough enough; you'll make it. Just hang on buddy."

A cheer went up above them. They looked up. Clay managed to turn his head far enough to see. Six GIs were raising the American flag on the peak of Mt. Suribachi. It was 10:20 A.M., February 23, 1945.

Clay's voice became stronger as he asked, "Isn't that one of my people? Isn't that one guy helping raise the flag a redskin?"

"Yes he is," said the medic. "I met him once at the foot of the mountain. I think his name is Hayes. . . Isn't that a beautiful sight? We made it guys: We did it. We took the damned mountain!"

"Rusty Red," whispered Clay, with great effort.

"I'm still here, Little Injun. I won't leave you until they get a stretcher here for you."

"We been good friends a long time, huh, Rusty Red?" Clay asked, his voice getting weaker.

"Ever since our famous battle in the chicken coops," said the redhead, smiling despite his tears.

"Rusty Red, my dream of being a warrior was a false dream. . . Not like I imagined. It was all wrong. . ."

"Right or wrong. . . I don't know. . .about your dream. But I say again, you are as brave as any warrior I have known, even back to our days at the Raft. You never backed down to anyone." Then he added, still crying unashamedly, "And now the warrior is going home."

Clay smiled at his friend and grasped his hand. The gunfire, the noise of battle, the voices began to fade and were gone. The sky was filled with a giant sun, and Clay could hear the voice of his grandfather, very softly, coming from the sky. It gradually grew stronger and louder. His grandfather was singing an old song of the *Dineh* that he had sung to Clay when he was a small boy:

> I walk in beauty
> Beauty surrounds me
> Beauty is everywhere
> I walk with holiness.

Walks Two Worlds smiled up at the bright sun and murmured to himself, "The Warrior is going home."

EPILOGUE

They were the rawest of recruits, most of them coming straight off the reservations of Arizona, Utah and New Mexico. Many were in their teens, a few only fifteen or sixteen. Most of them came from poverty, having never had indoor plumbing or the luxury of bathtubs, hot showers or the wonders of electricity. Only a few of them had much previous contact with the White Man and his world. These were the Navajo who became the Code Talkers of World War II.

They saw combat in the bloodiest battles of the Pacific Islands. Carrying their heavy radio equipment in addition to their weapons, they would call in air strikes, shelling from off shore guns and communication between fighting units, all in their native Navajo language. Their "code" was never broken by the enemy. Many years after the war, General Seizo Arisue, former Chief of Intelligence for the Japanese forces, was told that our messages were transmitted in the language of an American Indian Tribe. He replied, "Thank you. That is a puzzle I thought would never be solved." The Navajo code may very well have been the only unbreakable code in the history of warfare.

It is estimated that at its peak there were approximately four hundred code talkers. Many of them were wounded in combat. Seven were killed. Many received medals for bravery under fire. Major Howard M. Coner, communications officer for the Fifth Marine Division said: "Without the Navajos, the Marines would never have taken Iwo Jima."

Sadly, due honor was late in coming to the Code Talkers. The project was kept classified "top secret" for twenty-three years. The classification was dropped in 1968. The first Code Talker Reunion was held at Window Rock in 1971.

Doug Hyde, a renowned sculptor and Native American, was commissioned to create a monument to honor the Code Talkers. The ten foot sculpture was completed and placed in the Phoenix Plaza. It was unveiled and dedicated on March 2, 1989. Hyde says of his sculpture: "It depicts a young Native American boy with flute. Among many Native Americans, the flute is a symbol of communication and peace."

Hyde goes on to explain his sculpture: "I wanted to leave an impression of the gentler side of these people, like the kid out herding the sheep. That's exactly what most of them were before being a warrior. That's why I chose the lone Navajo boy playing the flute."

It is my hope that this fictional account as I have presented it, is another small tribute to the Navajo Code Talker.

---

[1] *Philip Johnston, General Vogel, and Colonel Wethered Woodward are the names of real people who initiated the code talker program into the Marine Corps.*